Horace Hills

**Constance**

A poetical romance

Horace Hills

**Constance**
*A poetical romance*

ISBN/EAN: 9783337048617

Printed in Europe, USA, Canada, Australia, Japan

Cover: Foto ©Andreas Hilbeck / pixelio.de

More available books at **www.hansebooks.com**

# CONSTANCE:

—A—

# POETICAL ROMANCE.

—BY—

## Horace Hills, Jr.

WILLIAMSPORT:

THE TIMES PRINTING HOUSE.

1877.

# INDEX.

—o—

# PREFACE.

—o—

The scene of the following story is laid in Virginia, during the summer and fall of 1781, the last year of the American Revolution. The historical events narrated are in the main true, though some slight liberties have been taken for the convenience of the narrative. Stratford House, the home of the heroine, is the old family mansion that once stood on the southern bank of the Potomac, in Westmoreland county, Va., supposed to have been built by Richard Lee, sometime during the sixteenth century. It was destroyed by fire early in the eighteenth century; but soon rebuilt, and now stands, a stately manor house of the olden time.

In conclusion, the author submits this little work, hoping that its demerits may be overlooked, and that it may receive some slight portion of that kindly favor so grateful to the heart of every writer.

# INTRODUCTION.

## 1.

Long years had passed.  Fair Peace, with gentle reign
Ruled o'er the land, in willing bondage held;
While, from the borders of her vast domain
Were'linked the golden fetters, that of eld,
Forged by the cunning wisdom that could weld
The souls of men by fire of eloquence,
Made of her sons' true hearts her sure defence.

## 2.

O land of happy memories! how blest
Of Heaven !   O land to patriot hearts how dear!
On thee, O sunny haven of the West!
From budding Spring, the opening of the year,
Till Autumn crowns her glorious career,
Doth nature, with unrivalled splendor, pour
Her choicest blessings from her boundless store.

## 3.

And sped to distant land, on eastern gales,
The news of thy fair Paradise; and came
Full many an argosy, with swelling sails,
Their lordship o'er the envied realm to claim ;
And plant their standards, in the royal name,

In soil to Freedom consecrate alone;
Who other sovereign aye refused to own.

### 4.

Then drifting clouds the brightness of her sky
  Began to dim, and distant thundering
Announced that war, with dread approach was nigh.
  And last, fair Peace, unsoiled her snowy wing,
  Flew back to Heaven's high courts, and wondering
Looked down, the while her pitying tear-drops fell,
If aught so pure war's tempest might dispel.

### 5.

But fiercely burst the storm, and discord reigned—
  Yet lived there noble hearts amid those days;
Who 'mid all change, unchanging still remained.
  For these, O, tuneful muse! I bid thee raise,
  In sweetest strain, thy loftiest notes of praise:
In name of Honor, and in gentler name
Of deathless love, through adverse fate the same.

### 6.

The unseen minstrel long had silent been;
  But at the well-known themes her hidden fire
Awoke once more; and trembling within,
  Like winds that breathe through an Æolian lyre,
  Grew deep and strong with passionate desire;
And to her sounding harp once more she sang,
Till rock and wood with sweetest echoes rang.

# CANTO I.

—o—

## THE MEETING.

### I.

The setting sun with level ray,
As all too short his welcome stay,
Paused, gilding with a fiery flood
High towering hills and bordering wood,
Where wound its way with babbling song
A mountain brook, that gleamed among
The emerald hills, a silver chain,
'Twixt upland height and lowland plain.

### II.

Where first the hilltops came to view
A noble boundary line they drew,
That arched the heavens with mighty span
To where the lowlier woods began.
These, in their turn, enriched the scene
With darker hues of rustling green ;

Then merged in meadows broad and fair,
Whose silken banners waved in air
Did homage to the passing breeze,
And nodded to the whispering trees.


### III.


The laughing brook here spent its force,
And holding still its wayward course,
Yet widened to a broader bed,
With sluggish current overspread,
Whose pebbly bottom gleaming through
Each nook and shoal revealed anew,
Where hid the angler's speckled prey,
Or shot like light upon his way.


### IV.


Here crossed a narrow lane, that wound
Far upward o'er th' uneven ground,
Till on the mountain's topmost height,
By copse and brush 'twas hid from sight.
No foot had trod its pathway bare
Since last the sunlight lingered there;
Nor, from the earliest gleam of dawn,
Had timid deer or startled fawn
Crossed the wide mead, or at the brink
Of the clear water stooped to drink.

But nature, undisturbed that day,
Had dreamed the golden hours away.

## V.

Now, through the richly glowing light,
A single horseman came in sight;
Distant at first, then drawing near,
And urging on in full career
His noble steed, that lightly flew,
As near, and nearer still he drew;
Crossed the wide brook with easy bound,
And galloped o'er th' uprising ground,
Intent to reach the distant height
Ere fell th' approaching shades of night.

## VI.

The rider's nodding plume and blade
Of war's pursuit confession made.
Not many years had passed him o'er,
Though manhood's fullest prime he bore;
And though life's care had left impress,
'Twas scarcely more than light caress
In passing; as her hand had stayed
Ere mark indelible was made,
And bade him still youth's honors wear,
Who their light weight so well could bear.

## VII.

Now up the steep ascent they pressed,
Nor paused to breathe, nor stopped to rest,

Until, the lofty summit gained,
His horse the rider lightly reined.
And leaping from the saddle stood
To view the leafy solitude,
Where nature's lavish hand displayed
What store her boundless wealth had made.

### VIII.

On either hand, like walls of strength,
The hills drew out their endless length.
Opposing ranges dimly seen
At distance were; while lay between
A fertile vale of wide extent,
With summer's growth luxuriant.
The brooklet from the mountain side
Swelled a deep river's flowing tide,
That through broad mead and verdant lea
Stretched onward to the distant sea.

### IX.

On nearer side, a rocky ledge
Sought with bold sweep the water's edge;
Then back retiring left a plain,
Or table, in the mountain chain,
That seemed by natural fitness made
For garrison or ambuscade.
Pursuing here his endless round,
A single sentry paced the ground.

Beneath, a mighty army lay,
Whose tents in orderly array
The level meadow dotted o'er,
From mountain range to sloping shore.

### X.

Anon was heard the soldiers' song,
 Whose chorus reached his listening ear,
Like Alpine echoes, borne along
 By varying winds, now far now near.

---

## SOLDIERS' SONG.

### 1.

When ceased the battle's roar,
War's thunders heard no more,
For briefest holiday,
Idly the soldier may
 Rest—idly rest.
Ring out a merry shout!
 Tell in gallant measure,
'Twixt strife the soldier's life
 Still is life of pleasure.

### 2.

When beats the light reveille,
Soldier and sentinel

Quick to their stations come,
And, at the tap of drum
　Stand—ready stand.
Ring out with fearless shout
　Challenge to the foeman!
At dawn with weapons drawn
　Stands each sturdy yeoman.


### 3.


Then at the trumpet's sound,
Shakes 'neath their tread the ground;
Footmen and cavalry,
Lancers, artillery,
　March—onward march.
Ring out inspiring shout!
　And with war drum's rattle,
Swell high the loyal cry,
　Signal for the battle.


### 4.


Now in the deadly front,
Bearing the battle's brunt,
But with undaunted will,
Bravely the soldier still
　On—presses on.
Ring out victorious shout!
　Tell the noble story;

'Mid strife the soldier's life
Still is life of glory.

### XI.

Low in the western heaven the sun,
Still lingering ere his race was run,
A flood of golden splendor poured
O'er the rich vale and teeming sward ;
Then sank from view, as loudly spoke
The evening gun, and straight awoke
The rattling echoes' sharper sound,
From hill to hill with quick rebound ;
As viewless elves that slumbered there,
Had waked to revel in the air.

### XII.

Scarce was the first loud echo heard,
Ere from its staff, like wounded bird,
That folds its wings and stoops to die,
Slid down the silken canopy,
That high in air, with breezy play,
Had floated since the dawn of day.

### XIII.

Then dimmed by distance came the tramp
Of warder marching through the camp ;
While hoarse command and clang of arms,
Rang through the air their loud alarms,

As watch was set 'gainst nightly foes,
Ere sought the soldier his repose.

### XIV.

Then night, with silver studded pall
Descended on the earth, and all
Its sounds were hushed, its voices still,
Save that the plaintive whippoorwill,
With tender, melancholy lay
Beguiled the darkling hours away.

### XV.

Now roused the traveller from his rest,
And to his further way addressed
His thoughts; the while his gallant steed
Slacked somewhat of his former speed,
Yet onward pressed with steady pace,
Not unfamiliar with the place.

### XVI.

The road soon wide and wider grew,
And tokens gave, though faint and few,
That hand of man had once essayed
Fair nature's handiwork to aid,
And keep with artificial care
The natural roadway in repair.
Here, trace of woodman's axe was seen,
Where stripped of all its vestments green,

Some lofty monarch of the wood,
That long in towering pride had stood.
Now prone on earth forgotten lay,
And crumbled into dust away.

There massive stones were widely strewn,
As if some Titan force had hewn
The mountain, and unearthed its store,
In fruitless search of hidden ore.
Yet piled like ruined castle wall,
That at no distant day must fall,
A few in loose confusion lay
Near ravine's edge, and warned away
The traveller's steps, who unaware
Might plunge in deep destruction there.

## XVII.

At length low copse and shrubs gave place
To trees, that rose with stately grace,
While high above, like gothic fane,
Their leafy arms entwined again,
Moved softly, at the gentle hest
Of zephyrs laden with the blest
Perfume of those night blooming flowers,
That sleep through day's long, sunny hours.

## XVIII.

Though dark the shadows of the night,
And Heaven bestowed but little light,

Yet myriad fire-flies lined the way,
And danced in evanscent play;
Like sparks from glowing forge that fly,
And in one moment live and die.
Then bright Aurora from the North
Led all her gleaming banners forth,
And piled the blazing Heavens with flame;
With glittering 'tongues that went and came;
And shimmering clouds that hid the skies,
While diamond stars, like houri's eyes,
Peeped through the luminous veil, to see
The world that slept so silently.

### XIX.

On through the fragrant forest rode
The traveller; while the horse he strode,
Conscious the goal was well nigh made,
Snuffed the fresh air, and loudly neighed.
For answer came, with lengthened sound,
The distant baying of a hound.
"Ha, Jura, well thy voice I know:
A faithful creature thou, although,
Thy days of active service o'er,
Thou'lt course the fleeting stag no more."

### XX.

He spoke, and reached an outer gate,
Where stood an aged man to wait;

Whom sound of footsteps summoned here,
To learn if friend or foe were near.
"Who comes?" "'Tis I, good Paul." "St. John?"
"The same." "Then all my fears begone;
That name is symbol of good cheer,
And thou art ever welcome here."

## XXI.

With ready hand the bolt he drew,
And let the weary traveller through.
He lightly leaping to the ground
Cast one impatient glance around,
Then gave his hand, with kindly word
To Paul, who scarce his greeting heard,
But stood, with wonder and amaze
Depicted in his steadfast gaze.

## XXII.

At length, "Scarce seems it true," cried he,
"That thou in life and health shouldst be;
For three days since we heard from far
That thou hadst fallen in the war;
And though we hoped, 'gainst hope, again
To see thy living form, since then
Have doubt and sorrow ruled each day
The tardy hours—but come ; away

To meet thine honored host; the road
Full well though know'st to his abode;
And I thy charger here will lead
Where rest and food, his well earned meed
Await." Then on with eager tread,
O'er a well ordered pathway, sped
St. John, while Jura, faithful hound,
Attended, and with frisk and bound
Expressive welcome sought to show;
But stiff with age, soon to forego
The task compelled, though scarce resigned,
Came panting slowly on behind.


### XXIII.

In stately height before, appeared
A noble mansion, that had reared
Its crest the proudest in the land.
Till war's all desolating hand
Plucked half its massive walls away,
That now in mournful ruin lay.
There oft the sound of music sweet
Had timed the merry dancer's feet;
And gallant men and ladies fair,
Had met in stately revel there.
But now that brilliant throng was fled;
And, like a city of the dead,
Its halls in silence seemed to mourn
The pomp and splendor, proudly borne

In days that owned the gentle reign
Of peace, with all her prosperous train.

### XXIV.

Yet not all given to decay—
The ruthless hands that plucked away
The northern walls, as shame had taught
Repentance, ere destruction wrought
Her work complete, one part had left ;
That of its twin companion reft,
Like sentinel, seemed watching o'er
A fallen comrade, now no more.

### XXV.

Here dwelt, in lonely grandeur still,
The mansion's lord ; whose iron will
Upholding truth with loyal zeal,
And braving death by fire and steel,
Him mark for wanton foes had made,
And lawless trespassers, who preyed
On whom to greater force must yield,
But shunned fair fight in open field.

### XXVI.

With him an only grandchild shared
The dangers he so boldly dared ;
And of retainers faithful few
Remained to render service due.

The rest their several ways had ta'en,
And some on battle field were slain.


### XXVII.

Now in the vaulted entrance rung
The soldier's step; wide open flung
The door, was Percival revealed;
Who, though the snows of age concealed
A brow deep lined with care, yet stood
Erect and firm, as in the wood
Some sturdy oak uprears its form,
And bids defiance to the storm.


### XXVIII.

With glance that kindly was, yet keen,
He viewed the stranger, and had seen
His bushy beard and well bronzed face
One moment, ere his eye could trace
Remembrance—then the well-known name,
In flash of recollection came.
"My son! almost as dear to me
As if my life blood flowed in thee.
Thrice happy welcome! for indeed
The old man's heart hath had sore need
To meet thee once again; for come
Misfortunes thickly; and though dumb
Before yon traitorous hosts, within
The mind's still chambers there hath been

At times deep sense of sorrow felt;
Though not on themes like these have dwelt
My thoughts too oft—but welcome now ;
And welcome yet again, for thou,
Like first bright'harbinger of spring,
Dost happy omen with thee bring."

XXIX.

Then ushered Percival his guest
Within, and turned with brief behest
To servitor, who at his call
Came forward from an inner hall.
Then to his son once more, "And now,
Amidst that bloody battle how
With life thou did'st escape, when fell
So many gallant men, first tell.
For even now 'tis scarcely clear
That though before me dost appear,
In thine own person ; whom to see
Again I scarce dared hope." Then he,
" 'Tis true I fell; o'erwhelmed by force
Resistless of the foemen's horse,
Who came like whirlwind, ere our line
Their scattered columns could combine
To stem the torrent. But reprise
Came swiftly ; for as eagle flies
To meet her foe, with deadly aim,
So on, with thundering chargers, came

My own brigade, who turned the tide
Of war, and scattered far and wide
Our rude assailants; left they none
Who could the tale relate, save one,
Whom prisoner there we took. Unarmed
By forceful shock, but all unharmed
Myself arose." "And thou didst make
Most narrow 'scape; e'en now awake
Mine apprehensive thoughts to hear
Its bare recital. But what cheer
With thy most noble general; fares
He well, who still so bravely shares
The thickest of yon fight?" His name,
Emblazoned on the scroll of fame,
Shines brighter every day. 'Tis said
By some within the camp, that led
By such a general none can fail
But in the battle must prevail
Our forces."

### XXX.

Thus St. John, and turned,
Where in the open chimney burned
A light, yet cheerful blaze; whose flame
Fed by the odorous pine that came
From woods near by, with grateful sense
Of fragrant warmth, not too intense,
Filled all the room. Through open door
Meantime, came servitors, who bore

A bountiful repast, displayed
On ample trays; which duly laid
Themselves retired.  A lighter tread
Succeeding, raised St. John his head,
And there beheld, not all unknown,
A youthful maiden, who, alone,
With graceful dignity advanced;
While from her eyes the light that glanced
Had somewhat of remembrance too;
As if his face and form she knew,
Yet scarce her memory could invest
With title of the stranger guest.

## XXXI.

Then spoke, with all a father's pride,
The host.  "St. John, the years that glide
So swiftly past, make ample note
Of their departure, as they wrote
Each year with added growth a line
To mark their flight; so, as decline
My years, of half their length beguiled,
Each lives again in this my child;
Whom thou as little Constance knew,
Thou dost remember?"  "Aye! 'tis true,
Right well do I," St. John exclaimed;
"And ever hath her memory claimed

Most welcome place within my heart,
That scarce from one so fair could part."

XXXII.

Then Constance, blushing, as she heard
His words of gallantry, averred
With all sincerity, as might
IIis faith avow some olden knight,
Made answer, modestly expressed:
"And to my mind, at glad behest
Of wakened memory, comes the name
That thou, mine old time friend, dost claim;
And though somewhat hath time his hand
Impressed on both, unaltered stand
Those kind remembrances, that trace
Of time or age can ne'er efface."

XXXIII.

As thus they spoke, from outer hall
Appearing at the door, old Paul
Announced a stranger at the gate;
Who, since the hour was waxing late,
With weariness and travel worn,
Asked rest and shelter till the morn.
" Admit him then," replied the host;
" Yet hearken, Paul, full well thou know'st
The life of peril that we lead;
Of his appearance take good heed;
Let nothing 'scape thy watchful eyes,

For in these troublous times surprise
Comes oft in friendly shape." Away
He hastened, and with brief delay
Ushered the stranger to the hall,
And welcome gave in name of all.


## XXXIV.

When first the soldier's form he saw,
His step was checked, as to withdraw;
Yet on the instant reassured,
As if to self command inured,
Advancing with uncovered head,
He graceful reverence made, and said:
" Benighted here I lost my way;
And, lest the darkness should betray
My steps to paths unknown, I gave
My horse the rein, and here, to crave
Your hospitality soon came."
" And that hath been a sacred claim
With me, since first myself had need
To sue for hospitable deed,"
Made answer to the stranger's quest
The host, with courteous word expressed;
" And though 'tis time of war and foe
From friend at times we scarcely know;

Yet shall my kindly care be free,
And ample as thy need may be."

## XXXV.

Scarce had he ceased, ere quick replied
The stranger, yet with stately pride:
"Nor seek I aught at stranger's hand
Save what mine urgent needs demand:
Rest, food and shelter, that anew
My strength returned, I may pursue
My journey; and though long unknown
This land to me, and I, alone,
With prudence may not now disclose
My name and errand, yet thy foes
Are mine." "Nor do I seek to know
More than thyself art pleased to show,"
Replied the host. "And now, that care
Thy wasted strength may soon repair,
Due preparation here is made,
And in the task ourselves will aid."

## XXXVI.

Then, with high courtesy that became
His reverend years, he first the name
Of Constance gave; then of St. John.
As him the stranger looked upon,
Again was checked his onward move,
As if he vainly sought to prove

Some feeling of distrust, that o'er
Like passing cloud returned no more.

## XXXVII.

Then seated round the ample board,
From well filled flask the master poured;
And as the host's kind pledge he made,
Each guest the generous tribute paid.
And lightly passed the social hour;
Each owned and felt its pleasing power,
Save that alone the stranger seemed
Oblivious, and like one that dreamed,
With brow o'ercast, in silent thought,
Remained; as weighty care had brought
Of deepest import to his mind,
Some theme that could not be resigned.
Yet oft his questioning eye was staid
On Constance's face, as if the maid
Sometimes had mingled in the train
Of thought that occupied his brain.

## XXXVIII.

And seldom could the eye of man,
Though fairest beauties used to scan,
More pleasing form or features see
Than hers; by Nature made to be
That rarer type of human mould
Whose graces from within unfold,

And blossom brightest when is nigh
Congenial friend ; whose sympathy,
Like summer sun's enlivening ray,
Calls forth new beauties every day.


### XXXIX.

Not long had she the mantle borne
Of womanhood; so lightly worn,
That now scarce more than child she seemed,
But for the graver light that beamed
At times, from eyes, whose depths could tell
The soul's deep history passing well.
Yet not all grave ; full well she knew
When to be gay, when pensive too.
Well read in wisdom's learned page,
Could reason like some hoary sage ;
Yet with her sex's dainty art,
Some subtle witchery could impart
E'en to the fluttering ribbon, where
It scarce confined her waving hair.


### XL.

Of care maternal early reft,
Her grandsire's sole companion left,
Till now she lived for him alone ;
And was her rare affection shown

By every art, that love could move
A daughter's willing heart to prove.


### XLI.

At length the silent stranger rose,
And pleading need of long repose,
Withdrew, where for his weary head
Refreshing couch before was spread.
Then Percival, "St. John, know'st aught
Of yonder stranger? for methought
His looks twice on thy features fell,
As if thy name he fain would tell."
"Until this night his face to me
Hath stranger been." "Then, sooth, hath he
Some likeness to an absent friend
In thee discerned; doth Nature send
Oftimes the like reminders—most,
When least expected," said the host


### XLII.

Then in long converse swiftly sped
The hours away, till silence spread
Oblivious mantle o'er the manse,
And slumber wrapped in dreamless trance
Its inmates—all save one, who paced
In silence to and fro, and traced,
With finger on the window-pane,
Two words, that one had sought in vain

To read; then breathed them o'er and o'er,
While pacing still the chamber floor,
Till, echoed like a weary moan,
The walls gave back, " Displaced—unknown."

### XLIII.

Then passing through the gallery wide,
At length he stood the couch beside
Where lay St. John in sleep profound.
In heavy folds the drapery round
Had hung, but stole the curtain through
The night air, laden with the dew,
Soft lifting from the soldier's brow
A fallen lock; revealing now
A scar his temple that defaced;
Yet for 'twas wound of honor, graced
His head more than could costly gem,
Though set in royal diadem.

### XLIV.

The wind passed by, unseen, unheard,
The parted curtain lightly stirred;
And shook, as when doth breast the storm
Some sturdy oak, the stranger's form.
Then turning from the sleeper's side
His couch he sought; nor sleep denied
Her solace then, but charmed away
All waking thoughts till dawned the day.

# CANTO II.

—o—

## THE BOWER.

### I.

The minstrel tuned her harp to gentlest lay ;
  Nor soared on tireless wing to loftier theme ;
But with the languor of a summer's day,
  Her vagrant fancies left at will to dream,
  As might with sweet forgetfulness beseem
An idle hour.  And whither led they then ?
O list the gentle dreamer's song again.

### II.

Now morn lifts up his radiant head.
With crimson canopy o'erspread,
High arching Heaven proclaims the day,
And vanquished night flits silently away.

### III.

As minstrel harp of old awoke
To arms, when morn of battle broke ;
So now, aroused by gentler lay,
Stepped forth to meet the opening day

St. John; to whose attentive ear
Came with low cadence, soft and clear,
The burden of a well-known song,
Borne on the freshening breeze along.

----

## SONG.

### 1.

Hail! The morn, with beauty laden,
Bringing joy to youth and maiden,
Now on rosy wings advances,
Scatters darkness with his glances :
    Veils her head
The silent night;
    Steals with tread
As fairy's light
    Far away,
    Conquered by victorious day.

### 2.

Earth exultantly rejoices ;
Wake her myriad tongues and voices,
In triumphant chorus blending;
While to loftier place ascending,
    Rears his head
The glorious morn ;
    Moves with tread
Like monarch's born,

Through the sky;
Mounting to his throne on high.

### IV.

At times some old, familiar air
Or tone, or scent of flower, lays bare
The past; and recollection brings,
On mighty rush of countless wings,
A host of memories, that arise
Like sunset clouds in Autumn skies,
So warm with life's own ruddy hue;
Then slowly, like the morning dew,
Or mist before the midday sun,
They pass, and vanish, one by one.

### V.

So now the song, a kindred strain
Waked in his heart, that thrilled again;
And back, like ocean's surging tide,
With force resistless, that defied
All barriers, swept each hurrying thought;
And to his mental vision brought
Swift glances of the past, when he,
Well used to art of minstrelsy,
The tuneful Goddess here had wooed,
When wandering forth in idle mood.

### VI.'

The vision past, like one that dreams,
And wakes from sleep, while scarcely seems

The present moment real, he stood;
Then turned, and toward a neighboring wood
His footsteps bent; in whose deep shade
Ofttimes before himself had strayed.
Not far he went, ere, as he held
Some fairy talisman of eld,
That guided by its secret clue
Straight to the spot he wished to view,
A sudden turn the source revealed,
Like Delphic oracle concealed,
Whence floated on the morning air
The harmonies that drew him there.


VII.

Beneath the trees, whose leafy dress
In all its summer loveliness,
Reflected back the rays of morn,
With thousand sparkles newly born,
The songstress stood ; and ceasing now,
Bent low beside an alder bough,
On which a dove its nest had made;
Whose downy fledgelings, undismayed,
Cooed soft delight, while scarcely stirred
From neighboring branch the mother bird.


VIII.

Well might St. John his steps arrest,
And gaze with wonder scarce represt ;

For could no lovelier vision grace
The sylvan beauty of the place;
And though last eve confessed her fair,
This morning she seemed beyond compare
The purest, brightest, that could claim
Her own, a mortal maiden's name.


IX.


Though lightly pressed his foot the ground,
Too soon her quick ear caught the sound;
And turning, like the startled deer,
Roused from her lair by sudden fear,
She met his gaze; and half in shame
For causeless fright, pronounced his name,
And gave him welcome while he spoke:
"When first this morning I awoke,
Came through the casement to mine ear
Soft strains that once I loved to hear;
(Though late too well have I been used
To battle's din and noise confused)
And brought sweet memories in their train,
Like violet's breath 'neath summer rain.
At once, obedient to the sound,
My steps directed here, I found—
A fairy, on enchanted ground."
Then, in gay humor, answered she,
"And to the fairy's bower with me

Now shalt thou come ; for here, to all
'Tis free; but her enchanted hall
Nor man nor maid hath ever seen,
Unbidden by the fairy queen.''

### X.

Then followed he where swiftly led
His woodland guide; who lightly sped
Through winding paths and hidden ways,
Well used to thread the forest maze.
At length was faintly heard the sound
Of water; glancing then around,
Her finger on her lip she laid,
And with mute gesture softly staid
His steps; then pushed aside a screen
Of matted vines, that hung between
Tall trees, and entered; close beside
He following, there a spot descried
That fairies well for haunt might choose,
Or secret hiding place to use.

### XI.

A single oak of giant size
Shot up, as if to meet the skies,
Whose myriad branches widely spread,
Made heaviest canopy o'erhead
Of curtained green, through which the sun
Cast slanting beams, that one by one

Their pathway marked, like bars of gold
On emerald ground : so knight of old
Might blazon on his crested shield
Device of gold on darker field.


### XII.

Around this monarch of the wood
Of smaller trees a few there stood,
So placed as if the hand of man
Designed for them some artful plan,
So even were the lines they drew
Of spreading circle, where they grew
From central oak on either hand.
So might some living monarch stand,
Surrounded by his court, who wait
To swell the retinues of state.]
Between the trees, like streamers, hung
Dependent vines, that lightly swung
With every breath of wind that strayed
On errant pathway through the glade.


### XIII.

From farther side its waters poured
A rapid brook, that fiercely roared,
As downward from a rocky steep
It plunged in one impetuous leap ;
Then foamed away on either side,
To meet not far below, in tide

That through the woodland bore along,
A tortuous torrent, swift and strong.
Within, as from its rocky bed,
A few loose stones, moss carpeted,
For rustic seats recumbent lay ;
While Flora's hand, as if in play,
Her fragrant stores had widely strewn,
With all the lavish wealth of June.

### XIV.

In silent admiration stood
St. John ; while she in merry mood
Then said, enjoying his surprise,
"Not oft is shown to curious eyes
This spot, my own retiring-place ;
Where, wearied in the toilsome chase
For learning, oft to rest I come ;
And seems it like some hallowed home,
Where, with unwonted power to bless,
Dwells source of purest happiness."
"And yet, methinks," St. John replied,
" That happiness should e'er abide
In breast so fair." "Ah, none can tell;
Hath grief at times cast wizard spell
Upon me, since my heart hath known
The ills of war ; and oft have flown
My thoughts to distant fields, dear bought
With blood of those who bravely fought.

But now, while briefly here we wait,
Thine own experience relate;
What battles thou hast fought and won,
What deeds of heroism done."
"Long were the tale, and short my stay;
For on this very morn away
We must depart from yon bright vale,
Where peace and freedom now prevail,
To lands where southern suns intense
Their glowing light and heat dispense.
Yet, Constance, ere again we part,
One tale there is that long my heart
Hath kept, till time on lagging wing
Fit opportunity should bring
For its relation. Soon 'tis told;
Yet its short length will I withhold
Should it prove wearisome." No word
Spoke Constance, as his voice she heard;
But once, with questioning eye she sought
His face, as if to read his thought;
Then on the ground her glances bent,
And sat, with listening ear intent.
One moment paused he, then began
His tale, and thus its purport ran;

XV.

" 'Twas where the balmy south wind blows,
At Christmas tide where blooms the rose.

There Eden's bird, of gorgeous wing,
Resplendent, like a jeweled thing,
From bough to bough, with airy tread,
Flits like a meteor overhead :
And orange groves, with fragrant balm
Fill all the air ; like holy psalm,
When on devotion's wings it flies.
And wafts its incense to the skies."


## XVI.

"There lived a maid, in whose pure heart
Nor sin nor evil e'er had part.
As free her life from thought of care
As birds' that skim the summer air.
Each day, more happy than the last,
So quickly came and quickly passed,
That scarce had waked the rising sun,
Ere his victorious course was run.
By chance came to her father's door
A stranger from some distant shore.
The old man welcomed him, as one
In likeness of his long lost son.
(Fighting in foreign lands he fell,
Nor lived the dreadful tale to tell).
Long time the stranger lingered there,
Cheered by his hospitable care,
And soon the little maid became
His constant friend, and learned his name,

That sounded sweeter when she spoke
Than sweetest music, that awoke
When bard of old his harp had strung
And loud its mystic numbers rung."


## XVII.

" Like cloudless calm of summer's day,
Too quickly passed the years away.
When fell the sun's intensest heat,
Far to the north they fled, to meet
The cooler gales that circling there
Revived again the sultry air;
Then came, nor further wished to roam,
Back to their sunny, Southern home."


## XVIII,

" At length dread sounds of war arose,
The nation armed to meet its foes;
And he, though stranger in the land,
With willing heart and ready hand
Went forth, to fight 'gainst foemen's steel
For his adopted country's weal."


## XIX.

" The maiden mourned, with childish grief
Their severed friendship, all too brief;
Then laughed again with joy. to see
The glittering pomp and pageantry

That rode in war's attendant train,
And wished him safe return again."

XX.

"Through all the soldier's busy life,
In camp, on march, 'mid deadly strife,
To cheer his lonely heart there came
The memory of one face: the same
From day to day; no change could mar,
Its glad, bright beauty; like that star,
Born of the sun's departing light,
That shines unchanging through the night.
And as each morn it came anew,
Still dearer to his heart it grew;
Till with the gentle memory came
The whisper of a saintly name."

XXI.

"Three years had dragged their length away,
There came one memorable day,
When two contending armies fought,
From early morn, till evening brought
It's friendly shadows, and concealed
From each the foe that would not yield.
The soldier, who a charmed life
Before had borne, fell in that strife,
Pierced by a ball, whose deadly course
Had well nigh reached of life the source.
All night he lay 'mid heaps of slain,

And strove to summon aid ; but vain
His feeble cry, until the day
Had chased night's gloomy shades away,
When welcome succor staid the tide
Of life fast ebbing from his side.
Then reason's light with flickering ray
Now went, now came, from day to day.
'Twixt life and death so even hung
The scale, that lightest breath had swung
The balance down ; but slow returned
The light of life, so low that burned.
Came back from shadowy realms unknown
The spirit that had well nigh flown
Forever.  With the dawning light
Of reason, came like angel bright,
Once more the same fair face that beamed
Upon the soldier, when he dreamed
Of home.  Enfeebled yet his mind,
Still in those lineaments he devined
A something strangely new ; a grave
Yet gentle look her eyes that gave,
While in their depths, untroubled still
By any touch of human ill,
There seemed, as it had buried lain,
Now rising into life again,
A purer, nobler soul than knew
The child, ere she to maiden grew."

### XXII.

Fair Constance heard, with bended head
And folded hands, the words he said;
While mantling blushes well confessed
What deep emotions stirred her breast;
As back her willing memory strayed
And each familiar scene portrayed,
That oft like well learned task, before
Her mind in secret had conned o'er.
And dimly, as beneath a veil,
Was mirrored in the simple tale
What scarce she could as truth receive,
Yet scarcely dared to disbelieve.

### XXIII.

St. John had paused, but now resumed,
The while a graver light illumed
His features, like the misty play
Of sunbeams on November day.
"The soldier from his bed at length
Recovered, rose: new health and strength
Came, like reviving breath at morn
Of life, to infant newly born.
His heart companion now no more
Her gentle presence as of yore
Bestowed, but seemed to distance gone;
Yet dimly seen still beckoned on,
Came to the soldier's bosom now,
He knew not whence, and knew not how,

Love, with her varying doubts and fears,
Her strength and weakness, smiles and tears;
Yet tenderly she nestled there,
As benison of saintly prayer,
That falls in some thrice-hallowed hour,
To bless the soul with unaccustomed power.
Then, with new purpose armed he came
Back to the olden home; his name
In tenderest memory found enshrined;
Each friend the same, each welcome kind,
And her's most kind of all; yet vain
Now seemed his love; his tongue that fain
Would speak, was held in mute surprise.
A woman's soul beamed in her eyes,
The child, the maiden, gone; as far
She seemed removed as some bright star
That men would fain to grasp." Once more
The soldier paused; but not before
His secret had the maiden guessed,
For deep within her own fair breast
Too well the lesson had been learned
To love. Yet whom? She slightly turned
Her head, no word to loose. St. John,
Who marked the slightest move, spoke on:

## XXIV.

"Constance, that merry maid art thou—
And I the stranger; yet, e'en now,

When most their eloquence I need,
My suit in words I cannot plead;
For stronger than I may control,
Speaks the deep language of my soul,
That armed with mighty love, to thine
Goes forth." He ceased; no answering sign
Gave Constance, as like beauteous flower
That droops beneath the summer's shower,
She sat; her hands still clasped, her head
Still bended; while all words seemed fled.
Almost her beating heart was stilled,
While every word he uttered thrilled
Its chords, as master hand had played
On some sweet instrument, that made
For harmony, till that blest hour,
Ne'er knew, ne'er dreamed its wondrous power.

### XV.

At length, with broken words and slow,
Came utterance: "Scarce I thought to know
So soon the mystery of love.
For, till long absence came to prove
My heart, each merry, idle day,
All unremembered passed away;
But memory faithful proved—and strong,
And in my soul to love, ere long
Was turned; for in thy heart is shown
A faithful mirror of my own."

### XXVI.

O love! if e'er on holy wing,
Descending angel comes, to bring
Some guerdon from the realms of bliss,
To link that brighter world with this;
'Tis when thine own soft influence steals
From heart to heart, and each reveals
To other, as with lifted veil,
    Where now annointed eyes may see,
In circlet of its hallowed pale,
    A world of untold ecstasy.

### XXVII.

Withdraw we then, with silent tread.
'Tis holy ground, inhabited
By spirits pure.  Ill it beseems
To mingle with love's early dreams
Thought of the world.  Our steps away,
Now leads the purport of our lay,
To different scene, that horseman bold,
In six hours' riding might behold.    ˙
Here lay a deep and dark ravine,
Where scarce, the towering cliffs between,
Could penetrate with cheering ray,
The welcome sun, save at mid-day;
When from sheer height descending down,
His beams first tipped the mountain's crown,
And silvering o'er a light cascade,

Upon its rippling waters played;
Then downward, with unbroken sweep,
Sought the sheer depth in one bold leap,
To light with unaccustomed glow,
The dimness of the vale below.

### XXVIII.

Here might be seen a scattered band
Of lawless men, who scarce command
Of leader owned, save that more bold,
His haughty spirit their's controlled
By deeds of daring, that defied
Their wildest moods, and roused their pride
In such a chief; though scarce they knew
If fear or hate were most his due.

### XXIX.

Some, shrouded still in heavy sleep,
'Neath influence of potations deep,
In silence lay: their morning fare
The rest had gathered to prepare,
O'er crackling blaze, that fitful shone
Their ever moving forms upon,
And on the rocks rude palisade,
In strange, fantastic shadows played.
Nor feared they of their hidden dell
That aught the rising smoke could tell:
Invisible, it passed away,
Long ere it reached the upper day.

Their well groomed steeds secure were bound,
Where'er convenient place was found;
And burnished arms were scattered o'er,
In varied heaps, the earthy floor.

### XXX.

In gloomy dignity, apart
Their leader stood; while o'er his heart,
As in a fateful mirror glassed,
A crowd of strange emotions passed;
And goaded almost to despair,
A nature, well inured to bear
Life's varied fortunes.  Rumor said
That, long before, he sought to wed
A maiden, who her choice bestowed
  On one, who till that hour had been
His dearest friend—aye, brother: flowed
  The self same stream their veins within.
One mother bore them; though each name
From different sires descended came.

### XXXI.

What friendship can sustain that test,
To offer what the heart loves best
On friendship's altar?  He was sprung
Of sires, who, gifted with the tongue
Of eloquence, and wise debate,
Had in the councils of the State
Won high renown.  His rival came

Of ancient race that lived in fame;
In England's royal wars that fought,
And, fired with sacred zeal, that sought
In distant lands, the Holy Grave,
From Turkish infidels to save.

### XXXII.

Now brothers' love to deepest hate
Was turned.   He sought to instigate
The maiden's sire that suit to spurn
His rival urged ; and more to turn
His rage against that rival, spoke
Of his high lineage.   Fiercely broke
The old man forth, and deeply swore
That none who name of England bore,
How'er remote, his child should wed.
Of Puritan forefathers, bred
In tents of their sternest school,
Himself deep hated kingly rule,
And bade his daughter now refuse
Her suitor, while himself would choose
One worthy of her heart and hand.
Regardless of the stern command,
A secret marriage sealed their troth;
But soon, perforce, revealed, on both
His anger fell; yet while he planned
Revenge, by fell assassin's hand,
Himself was slain : his wealth the meed,
That prompted to the murderous deed.

### XXXIII.

Now sought, with fiendish design,
His favored rival to malign,
The suitor, whose rejected claim
Still rankled, like the deadly aim
Of poisoned dart.  Like thistles, sown
How, none can tell, by wild winds blown
At random, fell in evil hour
A few light words, whose venomed power
Suspicion armed, the hated name
Of favored rival to defame.
He for his life was forced to fly,
And died 'neath Italy's soft sky ;—
So came report ; but not before
His wife, who with the child she bore
Departed.  Could such weight of ill,
In any human bosom fill
The measure of revenge, to sate
The demon of incarnate hate ?
None ever knew.  His heart was sealed
To human eye, and nought revealed
That passed within.  Ambition led
Through varied scenes with eager tread.
Success bestowed her brightest crown :
Came every varied blessing down,
On Heaven's most favored that descends ;
Who with impartial wisdom sends
To all alike.  Now groaned the land

'Neath dreadful war's oppressive hand
And well his bold, ambitious mind
For deed of battle seemed designed.

### XXXIV.

Not war his fiery soul could tame,
Whose never sated thirst for fame
Led on, through danger, toil, and pain,
The still receding prize to gain.
And fortune, e'en till now, had smiled
On him, who seemed her favored child;
But, at the last, with base defeat
Had dashed his hopes, and in retreat,
Himself, with followers that remained,
Had scarce this spot of safety gained.

### XXXV.

Well might the soldier chafe and swell,
And on the nights's misfortunes dwell.
His arms dispersed; his followers slain;
But half their numbers now remain :
And added to the deep disgrace,
Most keenly felt by mind, though base
And sordid too, yet whose vast pride
Had swallowed every thought beside,
The bitter memory of past deeds
Obtrusive came; whose baleful seeds
Sown and forgotten, now to yield
Their harvest growth began : like field

Whose fruitful soil all barren seems,
Yet with a buried harvest teems,
That into life, with sturdy might,
Springs upward in a single night.


### XXXVI.

Swift visions flitted o'er his brain,
And 'mid the oft recurring train
Of forms and faces, came there one
Who long had perished 'neath the sun
Of other lands; whose name was dead,
To him by whose own act was sped
The deed. At length, as loth to bear
The thought, with an impatient air,
And gesture of disdain, he said
His thought aloud : " 'Tis false! the dead
Return not from their graves: he lives
But in this troubled dream, that gives
Its coloring to my thoughts, Away!
Before the gladdening light of day,
Ye base-born visions of the night.
Begone! nor e'er return to fright
My soul with baleful thought again.
What ho! De Hass, hast through the glen
Yet heard Le Claire's shrill signal horn?"
" E'en now I hear its echoes borne
From far—and by the sound he fares

From Westmoreland. Would that he bears
Good news; for ne'er before such plight
Had been my lot, till yesternight."
Thus muttering, he his arms began
With careful dilligence to scan.
For well the temper of each blade
In that fierce fight had been essayed.

### XXXVII.

Long were the lingering echoes flown,
Ere on the mountain side was shown
An active form approaching near,
With nimble step like mountain deer,
Towards whom a murmuring welcome ran
Throughout the band, from man to man;
As every eye, with gaze intent,
The progress marked of his descent.

### XXXVIII.

The scout, for such the name he bore,
Like one who oft had trod before
The self same path, though scarce could spy
Its windings an unpracticed eye,
Soon cleared the intervening ground,
And reached the spot, with lightsome bound,
And to the chief his errand gave:
"Sir Henry* toward Manhattan's wave,
From Southern victory now speeds.
Report hath reached him of thy deeds,

* Clinton.

That have his commendation won;
Who bids thee, ere this day is done,
With all the force thou hast, repair
To Gloucester's Point to meet him there."
"Small force," with bitter tone he said,
"Is left. My bravest men lie dead
Along the sanguinary shore
Where Cappahossack's waters pour.
Long shall her waves the story tell
Of gallant soldiers there that fell."

### XXXIX.

He paused, with melancholy air;
Then said in lower tone, "Le Claire,
Hast aught of import now to tell
Of those in yonder manse who dwell?"
"Last night the son returned. We know
Him well for honorable foe.
And later, clad in friendly guise,
A stranger came; who to mine eyes
Appeared like one who long abroad
Had dwelt, now pressed his native sod
With gladsome tread." "Ah," Glenwood mused,
"It may well be: though long unused,
The foot on native soil may spring,
As light as swallow on the wing.—
And yet, the son; in arms hath he
Maintained his cause right valiantly;
And doth our honor well behoove

That knowledge of his further move
We gain ; but now in haste away,
Sir Henry's summons to obey."

### XL.

Meantime, long ere his height attained
The sun, St. John the spot had gained
Where he had stood at eve's decline,
And viewed the long, unbroken line
Of snowy tents, that lay beneath,
Reposing on the tufted heath.

### XLI.

When the last rays of sunlight fell
Reigned silence, as enchantress' spell,
With force invisible had sealed
Her hest on bloodless battle field.
But now the glowing pulse of morn,
  Roused to new life by radiant beam,
Cast off the fetters night had worn ;
  Leaped through her veins in gladdening stream ;
And waked the sleeping earth again,
As fair and beautiful as when
Even and morn became the day,
And reigned where chaos first held sway.

### XLII.

And waked, like living harvest, grown
From seed in earth's broad bosom sown,
That mighty army : tent on tent

O'erthrown, its teeming numbers lent
To swell the concourse. Soon the plain
With surging life, like ocean's main,
Storm tossed, appeared. Confusion reigned ;
Or seemed it thus, to mind untrained
In art of war ; yet with the thought,
As if some master mind had wrought
His will unseen, swift order came :
The countless legions, each by name,
Their standards sought; whose folds wide flung
Waved in the passing breeze, or hung
All motionless; like idle sails,
Deserted by the truant gales.

XLIII.

Then moving o'er the level ground,
Inspired by martial trumpet's sound,
The vast imposing cavalcade,
In glittering pomp of war arrayed,
Swept onward ; passed the mountain's bend ;
And turning southward, where descend
Broad Rappahannock's waves, passed on ;
And from the gazer's view were gone.

XLIV.

"A goodly sight: yet well I ween
Stern war yon soldiery have seen,
Who seem with gallant bearii g now
To make but sport of arms." "I trow

Thou speak'st but truth," St. John replied,
With all a soldier's native pride;
And turned, while with instinctive hand
He sought where hung his trusty brand;
Yet ere upon the hilt was laid
His ready grasp, the act was staid:
For in the questioner's noble mein
The stranger of last night was seen.


## XLV.

Acknowledging the grave surprise
That spoke from his companion's eyes,
"Scarce had I hoped," he said, "to find
So soon a comrade to my mind;
For when this morn from yon abode,
To seek my further way I rode,
I found that thou wert lately gone,
In whom to speed mine errand on,
Though scarcely known, my heart full well
Did ready confidence compel.
But since kind heaven hath thus ordained
We meet, my suit shall be explained
While fare we on: for echoing still
From battlements of yonder hill
The trumpet notes assail mine ear,
That well I reck thyself dost hear,
With stirring impulse to begone
Where glorious war doth beck thee on,"

## XLVI.

"Now by my troth," St. John exclaimed,
"Thy words the very thought have named
That filled my heart.   On speed we then,
While with attentive ear again
I list, if aught in honor true
With ready hand I now may do
For comrade's need:" "No irksome task,
But little at thy hand I ask."
An exile from my native soil,
A prisoner, doomed to weary toil;
But late returned, my worthless life
To aid my country in the strife
I now would give : say, cans't thou lead,
Where with my trusty sword good deed
Of valor I may show?" "Right well
I can ; and would that might dispel
Stout arms and loyal hearts, ere long,
These heavy clouds of war that wrong
Our country; that with generous hand
Returning Peace might bless the land."

## XLVII.

Then turning where a path, scarce seen,
So overhung with matted green,
Led through the wood, a different way
From that he followed yesterday,
And spurring on his mettled steed,
Through brush and brier he took the lead;

And galloped hard for many a mile,
Till gained a narrow, long defile,
That seemed to pierce the mountain through,
At length the bridle rein he drew;
And pointing forward, "Soon, said he,
Our army's van guard we may see.
At noon they halt one hour, beside
The Rappahannock's flowing tide.
Now may'st thou see its waters gleam,
Where glints the sunlight on the stream."

XLVIII.

The spot soon reached, they looked in vain
For sign of life: the open plain;
The silent stream that onward flowed;
Bush, tree, or mountain, nothing showed
That, since the morn was ushered in,
One living creature there had been.
Yet could they penetrate the shade
　That clothed the mountain, they had seen,
Mounted and armed, a cavalcade,
　That towards them came; whose sabres keen
Sent flashing back each truant ray,
That through the branches found its way.
Their well trained chargers noiseless trod
The pathway, where fresh springing sod,
Or softer bed of fallen pine,
A carpet made that gave no sign

Of falling footsteps.  Foremost, led
The wary scout, with rapid tread ;
Whose watchful eye ere long discerned
The horsemen, who their steps had turned,
And slow along the river's side
Moved downward with its flowing tide.

XLIX.

With silent move he checked the train ;
And touched the leader's bridle rein ;
While in low whisper he exclaimed,
"See ! yonder, whom but now we named,
St. John thou know'st ; but him beside,
Who doth his steed so proudly ride."
Yet ere he spoke had Glenwood seen ;
And scarcely from the scout could screen
The sudden fear that o'er him came ;
While 'neath his breath a well known name
He muttered :—"Now, but that I well
Persuaded were that then he fell,
I could believe 'twas he.  His name
Dos't know Le Clair, or whence he came?"
"Nought could I learn save that alone
He rode ; his purpose all unknown.
But see ! approach round yonder bend
Our foemen's horse :—they hither wend :—
Aye, let them speed : soon may be tried
Their mettle, who so bravely ride.
But haste we, lest our tryst should fail ;

On! on!"  Like leaves before the gale
Fly the swift steeds, and long before
Their foes have gained the river's shore,
They leave the mountain far behind;
And flying as they rode the wind,
Shape o'er the level ground, as free
As ships upon the boundless sea,
Their course, nor slack the gallant chase
Till Gloucester terminates the race;
And all draw rein, with flourish loud,
Where floats King George's banner proud,
In wavy folds o'er Clinton's tent;
Who thence reviews his armament.

### L.

"Right noble welcome give we now
To thee," Sir Henry said; "for thou
Art ever foremost in the fight,
When battling for thy sovereign's right.
And art thou here at needful time,
For came this morn at early prime
My trusty messenger, who bore
Strange tidings from the northern shore."

### LI.

"Two days ago a hostile bark
Sailed in their waters.  Nought could mark
Our watchful scouts that might betray
Her country:  Deigned she to display

Nor flag nor emblem.  Thence to land
A stranger came, who scarce the strand
Had reached, ere sped the vessel on
With swelling sails.  He too was gone;
And lost his course till yester e'en,
When he at Stratford House was seen.
Yet ere the morning was returned
That he as secret spy, we learned
Was come : and more; 'twas shrewdly guessed
That, if his secret were possessed,
He comes from France ; for much we fear
That she, who friendly doth appear,
Hath toward these rebels secret bent,
And seeks to aid their discontent."

## LII.

" Now, for I know no heart than thine
More loyal beats, thou canst divine
How in this matter thy good aid
May foil their plans so deeply laid;
For well thou know'st each winding way,
And crook, and turn, by night or day
To follow, with unerring aim ;
And well each hiding place canst name,
Where in all seeming safety hid,
An enemy, these hills amid
Might lie.  Here in this paper, see,
What information more may be

Of use to aid thee in the quest:
And, that thou lack not for the rest,
What means so e'er thou need'st, command:
They shall be ready to thy hand."

### LIII.

Thrice back and forth did Glenwood pace
Within the tent its narrow space,
And with contracted brow perused
The paper, while he inly mused:
"'Tis he, this morn I saw. The same
That in those troubled visions came
Last night, and filled my soul with dread
Of coming evil. Can the dead
Arise; or is't my coward heart,
That plays me now the traitor's part?
But yesterday, and to mine ear
Was strange the very name of fear:
And now;—but shame;—what'er may come,
Before the world my lips are dumb;
And none shall e'er have cause to say
That Glenwood dared not to obey
His King's command. On then! this spy
His best endeavors needs must try:
For if I win he'll rue the hour
He fell within Sir Henry's power."

### LIV.

The varied landscape now, anon
With shifting scene, moves slowly on;

And in the distance dimly shows
Where Rappahannock's water flows ;
And, resting on its flowery banks
An army, whose scarce broken ranks
Denote that here but short their stay,
Ere they resume their onward way.


LV.

Apart, in earnest converse stood
The two bold riders of the wood :
And spoke from time to time a third,
Who their discourse attentive heard ;
Whose broidered cloak, in golden braid,
The marks of highest rank displayed :
"Doth Freedom, now by dangers stead,
Her welcome give to all," he said,
"Who came, with valiant hearts to brave
Her foemen, and her honor save :
Yet first, thy name ?"  " Is Henry Lee."
" A name of noble ancestry,
And honored by illustrious men,
Who well could wield both sword and pen.
But can'st thou ought of kindred claim
In this fair land?"  " But late I came,
A way-worn wanderer o'er the main,
And found 'neath war's oppressive reign,
Old faces gone, old faith betrayed,
And in the dust my memory laid ;

Scarce ought that once I called my own
Is left." " Yet, but these foes o'erthrown,
If Heaven our arms shall please to bless,
And all such wrongs may find redress.
And thou, I well believe, hast fought?
And bravely, or that scar counts nought."
" Of years, I've battled half a score;
In prison languished seven more;
Yet still mine arm is true; my blade
Ne'er once its honor hath betrayed;
And gladly now myself would prove
How deep I bear my country's love."

## LVI.

The general mused; then spake in brief;
"Nine leagues from here there dwells a chief
Who wages lawless war: whose bands
Distress and desolate our lands;
Yet whom in vain to subjugate
Our bravest have essayed. But late
They met McPherson, and were slain
Full half their number; yet remain
The rest, who still in vengeful mood
New mischiefs plan. Were they subdued,
Might other conquests be achieved:
For but our country once relieved
Of this vile pest, might concentrate
Our forces all; and ere too late
One mighty blow at England aim

For freedom.   Had I thought to name
This morning, one who should proceed
In this emprise.   If thou wilt lead,
Three hundred horse shalt thou command;
'Tis the full number of his band;
And, but thou take, alive or dead
This chief, whose name hath terror spread
The country round, the gallant deed
Promotion and reward shall meed."

## LVII.

The soldier bowed: "Be mine the task:
Nor greater honor could I ask."
"Then on with us.   To-night we rest
In shadow of yon mountain's crest;
Where York's wide spreading vale doth lie;
And when the morning gilds the sky
We'll point the way, and speed thee on
With a brave soldier's benison."

# *CANTO III.*

—o—

## THE MINSTREL.

### I.

Unwearied time moves on, with laggard pace.
  The summer wanes: but still, from day to day,
With gentle dalliance lingers in the race,
  Till Autumn, chary of the long delay,
  Begins to don his festival array ;
And, like a royal monarch fitly crowned,
His benedictions pours on all around.

### II.

O happy season ! When could lovers tell
  More fittingly of gentle hope, and fear ;
Or breathe their vows of constancy so well,
  As when the changing season of the year
  Proclaims that all things have their season here,
And all things change, but love, who comes to earth
In mortal guise, but claims immortal birth.

### III.

The purple heather lost its bloom ;
The dying leaves with sweet perfume

Enriched the air; a mellow haze
Stole softly o'er the earth, and rays
Of molten sunlight, glancing down
O'er field and meadow, bare and brown,
Strove with caressing touch to charm
Sweet summer back to life ; and warm
Earth's bosom with life-giving breath,
For one brief season, ere she slept in death.

### IV.

Swift move the glowing hours ; and speed
More swiftly still, like mettled steed,
Unused to curb of bit and rein,
That flies like whirlwind o'er the plain,
Through Constance' mind the memories dear
Of new born hope; of love sincere ;
So new, so strange, that now it seems
Scarce real ; like those delicious dreams,
When to the soul's half waking sense
Soft music steals; and bears it hence
On rosy wings of harmony,
To some bright land beyond the sky.

### V.

Her love, long buried in her breast,
So deep, that while herself it blest ·
She knew it not, now woke to earth ;
And smiling from its happy birth,

Came forth and beamed upon her face;
And lighted with its own sweet grace
Her features, till they seemed to shine
With living beauty ; so divine
That men could almost worship there,
Nor deem it sin to reverence maid so fair.

## VI.

In distant fields her lover fought,
But gave the maid his every thought;
And wished, impatient of delay,
The slowly moving hours away,
That must elapse, ere they could meet,
And every fervent vow repeat.
And oft as messenger was found,
Whose duty, or whose errand bound
His steps that way, came missive dear,
The maiden's longing heart to cheer,
With pledge of never failing love,
That absence served more deep, more strong to
    prove.

## VII.

Each messenger, like noble guest,
Was lodged and feasted with the best;
And, lingering o'er the generous cheer,
Would oft recount to listening ear
Of curious maids, the deeds of might
Of those who passed unscathed the fight;

Or sadder tale of those who fell.
And then, in lighter strain would tell
Romantic tale of camp or field,
And all the varied joys that yield
The soldier's life; and oft some word
Of rumor vague, but lightly heard,
Was mingled with the web of thought,
In strange, fantastic medley wrought.


VIII.

At times these tales did Constance hear;
Who, prompted by her love, drew near;
If from the soldiers she might learn
Aught her dear warrior did concern.
Nor did they soon the maid forget;
But, with their boon companions met,
Recounting all, would roundly swear
They ne'er saw face or form so fair;
And whispered that their captain bold
(Might 'neath his banner be enrolled
All soldiers true), was fortune's son
Most favored now, for he had won
So rare a prize.  And thus it came,
That once the half-remembered name
Of Glenwood reached her listening ear,
With some strange hint that he was near
With hostile force; yet inly prayed
He who the story told, that aid,

In every hour of ill might come,
To shield the maid, her sire, and home.

### IX.

Through the bright summer's short career
　No idle days had Glenwood known;
For, haunted still by that vague fear,
　Now well nigh certain that had grown,
With zeal unwearied he pursued
His purpose; but in altered mood;
For, since that morn, when through the screen
Of mountain foliage he had seen,
One whom he then believed to be
His brother, by some strange decree
Restored to life, no chance had brought
Them face to face; though each had sought
The other; yet, with secret fear,
He felt, nay knew, the day was near,
When they must meet, as foes; recall
The bitter past—and one must fall.

### X.

On broad Potomac's banks had staid
His band, and now brief revel made;
As soldiers wont, who oft, between
The toilsome march, or battle scene,
Can lightly cast their toils away,
And spend an hour in mirth or play,
As weariness were but a name,
And life itself a merry game.

### XI.

It chanced that of their number, one,
Born 'neath the light of India's sun,
(Thus 'twas believed, nor could belie
His swarthy hue and kindling eye
The tale, though nought himself had shown
What country claimed him as her own);
But lately to their number came;
And few had learned his state or name:
But with the rarest gift of song
Endowed, oft would his tones prolong
The twilight echoes on the hill;
Or floating on the night air still,
Along the silent river glide,
And die upon the mountain side.

### XII.

He now, with many a roundelay
Beguiled the social hour away;
And loud each jovial chorus roared
His comrades, while they freely poured
Bright, sparkling wine, that once had lain
   In dusty cellars, hid from light,
Of wealthy colonist, long slain
   While battling for his country's right.

### XIII.

At length his single voice arose,
As milder theme the minstrel chose;

# Constance.

And thus the tuneful muse addressed,
Obedient to his comrades best:

## Song.

### THE FROST KING.

#### 1.

Glittered the sun on the bare hill side,
  Powdered with hoary frost;
Sparkled the country far and wide,
  With gems which the night had lost:

#### 2.

For the Frost King came, at dead of night,
  With his army, a gallant band;
And away flew every fairy sprite,
  To answer his quick command.

#### 3.

First to the meadows, with noiseless tread,
  And arrowy speed they went;
And a spangled carpet quickly spread,
  By the frozen dew-drops lent.

#### 4.

Back to the city they lightly flew,
  With curious turns and whirls:
Scattered the earth, as the night wind blew,
  With a shower of crystal pearls.

5.

Some roofed the houses with dazzling white,
  And frostily draped the eaves:
Some decked the trees in a vestment light,
  And daintily fringed the leaves:

6.

Others with fanciful pictures graced
  The windows: others again,
With marvellous beauty their frostwork traced
  O'er valley and hill; and then;—

7.

Away through the pale moonlight they flew,
  And vanished in upper air;
But the scene they left disclosed to view,
  Was a sight both strange and rare.

8.

The houses were roofed with sheety white,
  And spangled with wealth untold:
The window-panes glowed with a mellow light,
  And the streets were paved with gold.

9.

Glittered the trees with the hoary frost,
  Pencilled with delicate care;
And every breath of the night wind tossed
  A thousand gems in the air.

## 10.

'Twas magic work, by a magic hand,
  On the landscape far and near,
Like a crystal palace in fairy land
  Did the Frost King's work appear.

## 11.

Glittered the sun at the high noon-day,
  On the hillside, bare and cold:
Its morning beauty had passed away,
  Like a miser's dream of gold.

## 12.

Afar, to the snow-clad, icy north,
  King Frost, and his sprites had flown;
For when the rays of the sun went forth,
  They fled from his heated zone.

## 13.

But all night long, till the morning breaks,
  He reigns with his fairy band:
And when the sun in his brightness wakes,
  They fly to the spirit land.

## XIII.

As ceased the song, drew Glenwood near,
And spoke: " Now hast thou pleased mine ear;
For, sooth, thou hast a merry tongue,
And well the roundelay was sung:
But canst thou troll some gallant lay

Of lady, or of Knight?
For much I love of olden day,
  Of tournament and fight
To hear; and once myself in song
Some little skill possessed; but long
'Tis fled." "So please you, I'll essay,"
The minstrel said, "An old romance;
Though not has knight for many a day
Or tourney rode, or broken lance;
And oft do minstrel hearts deplore
That knightly deeds are heard no more."

### XIV.

He paused, of warlike theme made choice;
And thus, once more attuned his voice:

### SONG.

#### THE KNIGHT AND THE BARON.

#### 1.

The baron, in his lordly tower,
  High revel kept.
The maiden, in her lonely bower,
  Sad hearted wept.
On the field of battle slain,
Noble sire, and princely train;
Friend or kindred, none remain:
  And her lover, distant far,
  Bore the cross in holy war.

## 2.

There came a knight from distant land.
  'Neath eastern sun
Well had he wielded lance and brand;
  Honors had won.
Now he hastens, all to lay
At his lady's feet, and pray
That her gentle voice will say,
  What the warrior's meed shall be,
  Who returns with victory.

## 3.

Now, on the castle's outer gate,
  Loud summons pealed:
" Ho! warder; noble knight doth wait,
  Who on the field,
Where, before the red cross fell
Saracen and Infidel,
Did with single arm compel,
  From the sacriligious foe,
  Victory, and overthrow."

## 4.

" Ho! warder, throw the portal wide;
  Welcome we here,"
('Twas the baron's voice that cried,)
  " With bridal cheer,
Who in holy war hath bled;

Who returns, by honor sped;
For to-morrow's eve we wed
  With the gentle Gertrude Clare :
  Fairest of all England's fair.

### 5.

Dark frowned the knight, with blackened brow;
  " Baron of Lorn,
Who violates his sacred vow,
  Knighthood doth scorn.
Thou on holy cross dids't swear
Deed of battle to forbear
With the line of Angus Clare.
  Faithless friend, and recreant knight,
  Broken oath must thou requite."

### 6.

Flashed from its sheath the baron's sword :
  " Knight of St. John,
Of Angus' lands the rightful lord,
  Lorn hath but won,
By fair fight in open field,
That which Clare would never yield :
But for thee, thy crimson shield
  Nought shall aid thee in the fight :
  On thine honor stand, base knight."

### 7.

Then rang the steel with hardy stroke :
  Roused from afar,

Each echo of the castle woke;
Mimicked the war.
Frighted menials stood amazed,
On the fiery combat gazed;
But no voice nor hand was raised :
Braver champions, well they knew,
Sword, in battle, never drew.

### 8.

Now each his foe more closely pressed;
Yet nought prevailed;
Till pierced the knight the baron's breast;
Fiercely assailed,
Stooped his haughty crest and fell.
Haste! O knight to yonder cell,
And the weeping maiden tell,
How hath love's victorious sword,
Her ancestral halls restored.

### XV.

At random chosen was the theme;
But flashed o'er Glenwood's mind his dream
Of months before; and half in ire,
That means so simple could inspire
With thoughts like these a soldier's breast,
He becked the minstrel from the rest,
And said : " Canst thou, good minstrel, tell
Where I such knight may meet, whom well

Thyself hast sung? Not without cause
Such one I seek; who 'gainst our laws
Hath great offender been." "'Tis true,"
The minstrel said, "that once I knew
A knight like him this simple air
Doth celebrate; yet how compare
With him thou nam'st?" "It matters nought;—
In many places have I sought
And never found;—yet here delay
Intolerant seems. I'll on this day
Towards yonder manse: there hath he been;
And yet may lurk its halls within.
"What ho! De Hass, forth from this place
Towards Stratford House we go: but grace
Of one short hour remains. Bid all
Assemble at the bugle's call,
Well armed, and well prepared; for long
The march may be, and foes are strong,
And watchful: haste! bid revels cease:
Our errand is of war, not peace?"

#### XVI.

As rang the blast with shrilly sound,
Hushed was the soldiers' mirth around.
As if dissolved some magic spell,
Uplifted glasses quickly fell;
And brows grew dark and faces stern,
And eyes with flashing fire 'gan burn:

And swelled each soldiers' spirit high,
As if at welcome sound of battle cry.


### XVII.

As rang the martial sound again,
In even ranks two hundred men,
Who seemed uprisen from the ground,
So quickly had they gathered round,
In silence waited for the word.
To bid them on; yet ere 'twas heard,
De Hass stepped forward; " Sire, hath flown.
The minstrel : yet 'twas scarcely known,
Ere search on every side we made:
But, for we might not be delayed,
And time was brief, we found no trace
Of flight, nor yet of hiding place."
" How? Fled? The minstrel dids't thou say?
He dares not bide the battle's fray.
Fear speeds the coward: let him go:
Ne'er follower of mine may show
The craven when 'tis time of need.
On ! then, nor slack your utmost speed :
And shall this night ere long declare
How much we still can do and dare."


### XVIII.

Meantime a lonely figure sped
Along the river's winding bed ;

And turning from the water's edge,
O'erhung with nodding reeds and sedge,
Pursued his way, through brush and weed,
And tangled grass with added speed.
As on like fleeting deer he pressed,
One single thought his mind possessed;
From that marauding band to save
The aged man, who shelter gave
When he had sued, an unknown guest,
For hospitality and rest.
And came, with sweet remembrance, too,
The image to his mental view
Of the fair maiden, in whose face
Oft and again he sought to trace
Likeness of one, though long since flown,
That he had loved, and called his own.


### XIX.

While thus his thoughts were occupied,
His footsteps scarce he deigned to guide,
But followed, with unerring aim,
A path familiar as his name.
On every side around were shown
Scenes that in boyhood he had known:
Each tree his curious eyes had scanned,
And with adventurous daring planned,
For nests, or feathered prey to scale:
Each rippling stream, each well-known trail;

And hill, and vale, and all beside,
Of olden memories multiplied
The sum.  Yet o'er the wide expanse
Unheeding passed his careless glance,
To rest where loftiest height attained
A range of hills, now deeply stained
With glory of the midday sun,
Whose downward course was just begun.
There at the foot full well he knew
Three hundred waving pennons blew;
Three hundred lancers waiting nigh
At welcome sound of battle cry,
Rung from his lips, would mount and speed
Where'er himself the way should lead.
And as he strained his eager eye,
Some distant token to espy
Of his brave band, scarce wings had sped
More swiftly on his rapid tread.

### XX.

As when draws near some rock bound shore
The mariner, and hears the roar
Of breakers, while the foam flung high,
Warns him of hidden dangers nigh ;
So now, behind him stretched a plain,
By distance leveled, like the main,
While close before, the broken ground,
In angry cliffs and boulders frowned,

Where many an ambush might be found;
While still afar the mountain rose,
Like victor o'er her prostrate foes.

Still following on the tortuous way,
With wary tread, lest might betray
His presence to some foe unknown,
That lurked within those walls of stone,
At length appeared the watchful guard,
Whose challenge stern his pathway barred;
But ere alarum sound he blew
The minstrel from his shoulders threw
His cloak; doffed all his strange disguise,
And might the guard now recognize
His captain, Lee; who winding blast,
Cried, " Mount! my men; ride hard and fast;
On woman fair, and age, doth wait
Impending danger: soon too late
'Twill be;—mount! mount! brave men, with speed;
Delay not;—haste,—'tis urgent need."
Then to a soldier standing by,
" Good Harwood, with my message fly,
Nor seek thy gallant steed to spare.
To brave St. John my greeting bear:
Tell him toward Stratford now we go,
And thou the road we take shall show.
This ring be warrant of my word:
On! on! my bidding hast thou heard."

## XXI.

Then mounting his impatient steed,
O'er rock bound path he took the lead;
And marshaled on the open plain
His followers, a goodly train.
Then at the word away they bore,
Like ships receding from the shore;
Till, fading into distant blue,
The mount at last was lost to view.

## XXII.

Yet ere from sight 'twas wholly gone,
Far to the left was seen St. John,
With chosen band, who rode apace,
And soon beside them had gained place.
Each leader silent greeting made,
And, mingling in one cavalcade,
Their forces thundered down the path,
Like mountain torrent in its wrath.

## XXIII.

Since first they met, these two had grown
In closest friendship; though, unknown,
Each silent hid within his breast,
What yet the other partly guessed,
One secret. From his friend no word
Of Constance, Lee had ever heard:
For love, though oft unconsciously,
Its idol views with jealous eye;

Nor brooks e'en dearest friend to show,
What one alone has right to know.
And Lee, in turn, had ne'er confessed
Aught of the past; though unexpressed
By word, St. John some glimmering thought,
Still to its perfect form unwrought,
In secret often would review,
And half believe the truth he knew.
Now scarce Lee's messenger was heard,
Ere to the meet St. John had spurred:
Well knowing that the word he gave
Meant urgent need from one so brave.
And now, in briefest word was said
The story, as they onward sped.

## XXIV.

Could one from some commanding height
Have looked, had he beheld a sight
Most strange. Towards one defenceless home
Two swiftly moving armies come;
One winged by love, and one by hate;
And, love, alas, arrives too late.
Glenwood, though now with slower pace,
As all unconscious of the chase,
Had reached the once luxuriant plain,
By the same road St. John had ta'en;
When he, returning months before,
Had sought his early home once more.

No longer down the mountain side
Flowed the clear brook : its course long dried
By summer suns, now whitely gleamed
In one long drift of sand, that seemed
For natural highway made. Below,
Where once its waters used to flow,
Few pools and shallow fords were shown,
With idle weeds half overgrown.

### XXV.

Here, pausing for few moment's rest,        ·
Then up the mountain, breast to breast,
Through the long winding road they wound
And halted, ere suspicious sound
Could reach the inmates of the manse,
And warn too soon, of their advance.
Here Glenwood skilfully disposed
His force on every side, and closed
Each avenue, whence might retreat
Unseen, the foe he hoped to meet.
Yet still concealed his force he kept,
'Neath woods, with branches low that swept.

### XXVI.

Then, riding forth with chosen few
He with his bugle summons blew ;
Like one at some old castle's gates
On embassy, who parley waits.

Scarce had the shrilly summons died
Ere stood the massive portals wide;
And Percival, like feudal lord,
Confronting some rebellious horde
Of vassals, stood, yet deigned no word,
Until their errand he had heard.
" In England's name we now demand
A certain rebel at thy hand.
Who here hath been concealed we know;
As thus our warranty doth show.
Him but surrendered, by decree
Of Royalty, thou may'st be free
As heretofore.   If thou refuse,
War's utmost terrors thou must choose."


### XXVII.

Spoke Percival, with noble pride;
" No rebel in these walls doth hide.
Who needs my hospitable care,
Or friend, or foe, commands it e'er
Beneath my roof hath couch been spread
For many; at my board have fed
Full many more.  Estate or name,
In these sad times to ask, were shame
As freely as they come, they go;
Nor aught I ever seek to know."
" 'Twere well if thou his name hadst learned,
Whom we demand."  Glenwood returned;

For hangs a traitor's name o'er thee,
In that thou'st harbored Henry Lee."

### XXVIII.

The swords from fifty scabbards flew:
And loud and wild the tumult grew,
As voices fierce with rage declared,
"Down with the traitor who hath dared
Our hated foemen's cause maintain;
Down! down!—Scarce could the cry restrain
Their leader's voice; whose stern command
Checked the rude clamors of his band,
And bade their ready blades be sheathed;
Who, though defiance still they breathed
Reluctantly obeyed. Around,
For the loud uproar more profound,
Fell silence, as awaited all
Word of defence from Percival.

### XXIX.

Brief time elapsed ere word be spoke:
While o'er his features swiftly broke
A lightning glance, where scorn and pride.
Like envious rivals to decide
For mastery strove; and speaking low,
With words at first constrained and slow,
Then urged by passion's rising force,
Like turbid torrent's headlong course;

"Call ye him traitor," then he said,
" Who for his country's honor bled,
When in her infancy she drew
But feeble breath ; and as she grew
And sought 'mid nations of the earth
Her rightful place, true to his birth,
Pledged fortune, honor, faith and fame,
To keep unsoiled her spotless name ?—
If this be treason, then indeed,
Thrice branded traitor be my meed."


### XXX.

Like hoary prophet, who of old
Some sin denounced, or wrath foretold ;
While the hushed multitude, in awe
Half doubted if the form they saw
Where man or spirit; he, inspired
With patriot zeal, almost had fired
Their bosoms with the glorious theme ;
But waked as from delusive dream
Loud murmurs rose, and spake their chief:
"Thy words are fruitless; time is brief;
With feeble age we will not fight,
Nor weigh vain questions.  For our right,
'Tis our commission from the King,
This rebel, and this spy to bring ;
And his command must be obeyed,
Though thou our warrant dost evade.

Go, thou, De Hass, and Hargrave too;
Make speedy search the mansion through.
If him we seek within is found,
One blast upon thy bugle sound,
And guard him well ; while to thine aid
We hasten." Scarce one step had made
De Hass and Hargrave, ere to stand
Bade Percival, with stern command :
"Came ye as strangers to my door,
Who needed succor, should my store,
With generous hand be freely spared,
And with the needy traveler shared :
Then freely might ye enter here
As summer rays, that warm and cheer.
But come ye here in hostile hour,
I bid you stand. Mine arm its power.
Hath nothing lost since I could weld
Thrice weightier sword on battle field,
Than ye, degenerate sons can bear."
Half awed by his commanding air,
The soldiers paused in their advance,
And, on the moment, as by chance,
From her apartment she had heard
Discordant sound of threat'ning word,
Beside her grandsire Constance stood.
E'en roughest men, in warlike mood
To woman's power allegiance own ;
And with a grace before unknown,

Bow to the power of innocence,
And wish their guilty passions hence.
So now, at sight of one fair face;
Its youth, its innocence, and grace,
Fled the fell purpose they had sought;
And every soldier there had bought
By desperate valor, from her eyes
One glance, and deemed it fair reprise.

### XXXI.

'Twas picture that a painter's art
Might well, with cunning skill impart
To canvas. Seemed as strange, wierd spell,
From source unknown, upon them fell;
And, for brief moment holding sway,
All life and motion charmed away.

### XXXII.

The stately manse, like castle gray;
The lordly man, who kept at bay
His foes; the gentle, shrinking maid,
Who clung to him, as half afraid;
The group of soldiers near who stood;
And those more distant, near the wood,
Who, half concealed beneath its shade,
The outlines of the picture made;
Now lighted by the golden ray,
That oft attends the closing day.

### XXXIII.

While thus the soldiery stood mute,
And Glenwood sat irresolute,
The scout was seen ; who closely pressed,
And him in undertone addressed :
" But now I saw on yonder plain,
Wend hitherward, a goodly train.
'Twere well short parley here to hold ;
For are they riders swift and bold ;
And though but little could devine
Mine eye, 'tis force exceeding thine."
The spell was broken. Quick returned
The former boldness he had learned
So well. " No further to invoke,"
'Twas thus to Percival he spoke,
" Thy loyalty we'll now essay,
Which thou hast well approved this day ;
But thou, as hostage must away
With us :—yet banish thought of fear :
For art thou much in peril here,
And with sure conduct we'll attend,
To harbor safe ; where to amend
Discourteous seeming, thou may'st bide
Securely, whatsoe'er betide."
At once, obedient to his hand,
Emerging from the woods, his band
To Percival, amazed, revealed
Their numbers : for before concealed

By shade and distance, he had seen
Scarce more than those, who, on the green,
In number few, had stood before,
Demanding entrance at his door.

### XXXIV.

From every feature flashed surprise,
And scorn he sought not to disguise. .
" And doth your chief an army send,
One aged man to apprehend?
Now were I armed, yet should ye say
Which most the coward showed to-day."
Glenwood, though wincing at the taunt,
Yet passed it by as useless vaunt;
And for the journey bade prepare
The maiden and himself; with care
But with all speed, that yet the day
Might speed them far upon their way.

### XXXV.

Though still his haughty spirit burned,
No answer Percival returned;
Nor further converse did he deign,
Since all resistance seemed in vain;
But proud as monarch still, withdrew,
And after brief delay, anew
Returned, and gave the gentle maid,
Who for the journey now arrayed
Appeared, his care her steps to aid.

### XXXVI.

Her own slight palfrey Constance rode,
And Percival the charger strode,
That him in earlier days had borne
In many a chase with hound and horn.
Then Glenwood bade the signal sound,
And on the slow procession wound;
Till gathering speed, and riding fast,
The hall and western wing they passed,
And vanished, as the sun went down
Behind the mountain's golden crown.

# CANTO IV.

—o—

## THE DISCLOSURE.

### I.

The dewy airs of night, perfumed with flowers,
  Whose drowsy heads her influence obey,
Fanned with their gentle breath the sleepy hours,
  And sped them noiseless on their shadowy way;
  And, as with lingering tread withdrew the day,
Soothed with her sweetest lullaby to rest,
Earth's fairest children, on her own fair breast.

### II.

Then rose with crescent light, her horns low bent,
  The moon, slow creeping up the eastern sky :
And looked with searching ray, as if intent
  To bless the sleeping earth ; then mounting high,
  As all her former glory casting by,
With still increasing splendor gathered round
Her silvery mantle, sweeping to the ground.

### III.

Dimmed by the splendor of her glowing tire,
  The lesser*stars, before that countless glowed,
Once more to realms invisible retire ;
  While she, bright empress of the heavens rode
  On cloudy chariot through her bright abode ;
Attended by two planets, that remain
Sole consorts worthy her imperial train.


### IV.

Now through yon copse, see, where uncertain rides,
  As heedful of the way, a silent train ;
And far before, with fleeter footsteps glides
  Another, o'er the shadows of the plain :
  And further still two watchers, who remain
In converse, while their drowsy comrades sleep ;
And far into the night their vigils keep.


### V.

Scarce one short league had Glenwood gained,
While his pursuers hotly strained
To intercept his lagging flight,
Ere the two foremost came in sight ;
And reined their foaming steeds before
The now deserted mansion's door ;
While their swift followers gathered near
In silent groups. Had thought of fear

Ne'er blanched the cheek, nor chilled the breast
Of either; yet, with lips compressed,
And boding eye, and darkened brow
Each looked his fear; and neither now
To meet the other's look could bear,
And see his own reflected there.
But leaping to the ground, St. John
Unsheathed his sword ; and bidding on
His followers, as with trumpet call
To storm some leagered city's wall,
Rushed at the massive door, that swung
On easy hinge, as fiercely rung
His sword hilt on its panelled frame.
On, following fast, his soldiers came,
Whom quick command directed where
To search ; while up the oaken stair,
He passed; through hall and gallery wide,
Through open door on either side ;
Yet found no token that could aught
Reveal of those he vainly sought.

### VI.

Each empty room, with hollow tone,
Gave back the echo of his own,
As ever with increasing fear
He called and listened.  Could they hear
Who but so late inhabited
The lonely manse, how quick had sped

The answer back.  How quick had turned
On fleeting foe his wrath that inly burned.

### VII.

Nor he alone, with fever'd rage,
Chafed like the lion in his cage.
Lee, who no less of zeal displayed,
Though more composed, his search had made
As one who knew the ancient manse
In every part; and with keen glance
Each nook and corner had explored,
With many an ancient relic stored.
But baffled here, abroad, where spread
The ample lawn, his steps were led;
Where, in the twilight falling fast,
Each object dimly seen, o'ercast
With shadow, he his search pursued,
And reached at last the friendly wood,
On rear and flank that guardian stood.

### VIII.

A long neglected road, he knew
Here pierced its sombre shadow through,
And recent footmarks deep impressed
Confirmed what he before had guessed.
Ere he had turned to summon nigh
His followers, met his searching eye
A ribbon, by the branch that swung
Of straggling bush that overhung

The path. Scarce was the token found,
Ere echoed to his bugle's sound
The stilly air, and came anon
His ready followers hastening on,
Who, marshalled near the stately hall,
Awaited but their leader's call.

### IX.

As way worn traveler listening, hears
Some distant sound of life, and fears
It may be foe; e'en while he mends
His pace, with earnest hope for friends:
So thousand hopes and fears, that passed,
As in a magic mirror glassed,
Within, now with alternate sway
Gave coloring to his fancy's play.
Hope that some bold, adventurous deed,
Or force of arms, or greater speed,
From foeman's ruthless hand might spare
The aged man, and maiden fair:
Fear that the desperate foe, pursued,
Their utmost efforts might elude ;
And far beyond their succor bear
The prize, 'neath foreign power to share
The sorrows of a captives' doom ;
Or find a refuge in the tomb.
These thoughts, and more, with rapid pace,
Had power in instant's time to trace

Their characters within his soul,
Like pen of scribe on parchment scroll;
And armed for desperate deeds of might,
In sacred cause of love and right.

### X.

While thus he thought, rode at his side
His followers; and impatient cried
St. John, who foremost in the train,
Now seized his comrade's bridle rein,
"Which way! which way! how rides the foe?
Speak quick if thou hast aught to show;
Time presses!"  Lee the ribbon showed,
And pointed with his sword: "The road
Hath not been used for many a day
Till now; yet could I find the way
At darkest midnight of the year:
Then haste we on nor dally here.
St. John and I the way will lead:
The rest close follow; but with speed
That caution rules, for well the foe,
Whom we pursue each wile doth know,
And artifice to 'scape pursuit:
Then, save command, let all be mute."

### XI.

Then spurring through the open glade,
He plunged into the deepening shade;

And, following two by two, close pressed,
In long and winding train, the rest.
The road was level for a space,
But thickly wooded; scarce could trace
Of twilight, still that feebly glowed,
Pierce through the shade. Still on they rode,
With steady pace, and even line.
At length the way, with slow decline,
Towards lower level to descend
Began; and wound with frequent bend,
Till reached the lowland, straight and free
It stretched, as far as eye could see.

### XII.

Though Glenwood still held slower way,
At Stratford House the forced delay,
And search prolonged, had won bim time
   To pass the Rappahanock o'er,
And by a secret path to climb
   The bluff that skirts its southern shore.
His followers here, with busy care,
For nightly shelter to prepare,
Their several occupations plied;
While he, attended by his guide,
Sought where the cliffs o'erlooked the tide;
And stood, like Highland chieftain now,
Upon the bare and rugged brow,
Surveying, with a glance as keen
As eagle's, the impressive scene.

### XIII.

The crescent moon, with silver light
Relieved the blackness of the night;
Yet not unveiled its deeper shade,
Where undulating vallies made
Long rifts; almost that rose and fell,
Now light, now dark, like ocean's swell.
The river, from its distant source,
Unwinding slow its sinuous course,
Upon its wide spread surface bore
The outlines dim of either shore;
Whose rugged hills their shadows gave,
Reflected on the glittering wave.
No sound disturbed the silent air,
Nor sign of life was seen; save where
Fled o'er the plain in wild career,
By fear pursued, some startled deer;
Then, like some phantom of the night,
Swift vanished from the gazer's sight;
While still more silent silence seemed:
As if, in slumber, one had dreamed,
And startled from his sleep, half rose;
Then sank, more deeply still, to soft repose.

### XIV.

Long silent Glenwood stood; then turned,
And to his guide; "The truth hast learned,
How are these northern armies led?"
"'Tis still in doubt," he, answering said:

" Rumors are rife that south they wend,
And have commandment to attend
The Marquis;* who, too well we know,
Hath proved no despicable foe.
Yet letters have been seized that tell
Of northern enterprise as well ;
That deeming further conquest vain
On southern soil, they still remain
To guard Manhattan." " Hast thou heard
That Count De Grasse hath pledged his word
To reach the waters of the bay
From Indies, at an early day ;
With six and twenty ships of line,
And other forces, to combine
In their behalf?" " That rumor too
Is rife, and much I fear, is true.
Yet hath Cornwallis at command
Abundant forces, to withstand
Combined assault by sea and land :
Though well his bravery may be tried,
For must we soon the issue bide."

XV.

" It may be so;—but list !—a sound
As if an army pressed the ground.
It louder grows ; as through the trees,
Portending storm, the freshening breeze
Doth sweep.  Now, on the farther side,
See ! one by one, three horsemen ride :

*Lafayette.

And now a fourth; and follow more;—
But mark you well who rides before:
The nameless stranger thou didst show
On that same shore three months ago:
Mine enemy; whom, since that day
I've sought:—but soft:—they come this way;
And see, beside the first now rides
A second, whose black charger glides
Like phantom steed that shuns the light.
He bears St. John. In fiercest fight,
Oft have our swords their cause maintained;
Yet neither have the battle gained.
And now they seek for passage o'er
The waters, and, as one before
That oft had crossed, the first doth lead:
'Twere well be on our guard: with speed
Go thou, Le Claire and bid De Hass,
With twenty men, to guard the pass
By which we came. Should it be known,
But little mercy need be shown;
For could we bar the passage long,
Against assailant trebly strong."


XVI.

The river passed, and gained the land,
Could Glenwood hear the quick command
Of " Forward," as with swifter pace
They galloped o'er the open space,

And halted 'neath the rugged height,
Where he, secure from treacherous light,
'Neath friendly screen of branch and leaf,
Could watch their further move. 'Twas brief:

## XVII.

The road, dividing here, became
Two separate paths ; though scarce such name
Was just ; for had thick undergrowth
Almost obliterated both ;
But, struggling through encroaching wood,
That more and more the way withstood,
They met once more in open road,
Whose smoother passage onward flowed,
As mountain streams, through narrow gorge
Opposed by rocks, a channel forge ;
Till, toil and fury spent, they gain
In one broad stream the level plain.

## XVIII.

Short converse held the leaders two ;
Then each his followers withdrew,
And sought, by different path, a way
Up the steep cliff where Glenwood lay :
Who now withdrew, and swift retraced
His steps, to where his guard was placed.

## XIX.

Well had he said that soldier bold
'Gainst treble foe the place could hold.

For reared by Nature, walls of stone,
Now loosely piled, now overthrown
In fragments huge, with rugged front
Opposed their threat'ning strength ; like brunt
Of serried weapons in the fray,
That bars advancing victor's way.
A hidden inlet, to the keep,
By path circuitous and steep,
Gave entrance ; but accustomed'eye
Alone the opening could espy ;
For well by clinging vine 'twas hid,
That swept the rocky pyramid,
And hung in gay festoons entwined,
Where'er its roots support could find.

### XX.

When Glenwood reached his post, had Lee,
Close followed by his cavalry,
Just reached the spot, where if were made
Assault, his life had dearly paid.
But all unconscious that so near
Was serried rank of blade and spear,
He, to his second in command
Said, with slight gesture of his hand,
" These rocks might shelter well afford,
Or secret hold, to some wild horde ;
Who like the mountain'goat, secure
Could leap or cling, with footing sure."

Glenwood, the voice that once had stirred
His inmost soul, in silence heard :
Yet came its long-lost influence then,
And o'er his softened heart again
Swept as of old, while riding on,
In slow succession, one by one,
Three hundred stalwart troopers passed :
But all had vanished ere was seen the last.

### XXI.

Then spoke De Hass, in tone suppressed ;
" Marked you the token in his crest ?
For, by my faith, 'twas ribbon rare,
That late I saw our lady wear.
Most like, ere we had left the manse
'Twas lost, and by some evil chance
Was found by him, who guessed our way,
And now pursues." " What could betray
Our presence there ?  When yestermorn
Our march began, no spy had borne
The tidings to St. John or Lee,
Of our long journey's destiny."

### XXII.

" Yet ere that journey had begun,
Our numbers lessened were by one."
" How ?  Follower of mine had fled ?—
The minstrel !—Aye, on his base head
Discovery rests. 'Tis well unknown

He came, or had his tidings flown
To other ears than he designed.
But, now their purpose is divined,
We'll means employ to wing their speed,
And on some fruitless errand lead,
Until our hostages we place
Within the Royal lines: then, grace
Of circumstance themselves may choose,
Nor we their challenge will refuse."

XXIII.

" How bears our prisoner fair the way?"
" As born of noble blood, to say
Her thought she scorns: but well I guess,
For actions more than words express,
That for her sire her deep concern,
Small leisure gives her mind, to turn
To other thoughts." " Soon we must hence,
And bear them to the strong defence.
Of York ; whose armed walls may frown
On foes like these defiance down.
Yet till good distance they have won
We'll rest, and with the rising sun
Depart. Bid all take brief repose,
Save needful watch, but not disclose
Our plans."

XXIV.

Meantime had joined again
St. John's and Lee's divided train,

And onward with unflagging speed
Urged their pursuit.  At length to heed
'Gan Lee, his followers urgent need,
And thus his captain made protest;
" So please you, sire, our steeds must rest;
For have they held unbroken way,
Almost since noon of yesterday ;
And for our further march 'tis need
Our strength should be renewed."  "Indeed,
He speaks but truth; how says't St. John ?"
" Unwearied would I journey on
Till gained our end; but for the good
Of all I yield.  In yonder wood
I know a glade where water flows ;
There may we halt for such repose
As time allows; for morning's light
Now follows hard upon the night."

## XXV.

The glade was reached ; the tents were spread ;
The faithful steeds were groomed and fed:
While, o'er the crackling blaze prepared,
Their homely meal the soldiers shared.
Then, with brief orison expressed,
Wrapped in his cloak, each sank to rest.

## XXVI.

O sleep ! they gentle boon who craves
Must earn the right to claim it.  Slaves,

Whose toil but little respite knows,
Taste the sweet blessing of repose,
And dream of bliss that care denies,
In this dull world their waking eyes.
Yet powerless thou at times to charm
The soul ; or of dull care disarm
The mind;—for while the soldiers slept,
Unceasing watch the leaders kept,
And paced with ever restless stride
Before the camp fire side by side ;
For anxious care forbade them rest,
And dull foreboding each oppressed.

## XXVII.

At length spoke Lee, " Some demon, sure
Doth desecrate the night so pure,
Whose shadow foul doth to my heart
Some dull, oppressive sense impart,
Of what, I scarcely know." " And I,
As if some strange event was nigh,
The same oppression share ; but sleep
All effort mocks, and while we keep
Our watch, my thought doth often turn
To thee; and fain myself would learn
More, should it please thee more to show,
Of thine own life, than now I know :
Not idly curious, but as one
Who of heroic action done

Hath heard, and now like eager youth,
Burns with desire to know the truth."

### XXVIII.

Long paused his comrade ere he spoke :
Then, as some secret thought awoke,
He turned, and thus St. John addressed,
  In accents stern, yet faltering still,
As if some secret grief oppressed,
  And shook the firmness of his will :
" Had I no thought that human ear
The story of my life should hear :
Yet, for I call thee friend, who ne'er
Had hoped with man again to share
Kind interchange of friendly deed,
Its secret history thou shalt read,
And in its sadness well mays't say
How he the penalty doth pay,
Who yields to passion's blinded sway."
He paused, and leaning 'gainst an oak,
While stood his comrade near, thus spoke :

### XXIX.

" Born where the sun's intensest ray
Draws out to endless length the day,
My nature owned his fierce control ;
And struggled in mine infant soul
A spirit, whose impetuous thought
Quick to the birth its impulse brought ;

And flashed to life, with lightning speed,
Each ill begotten word or deed.
To manhood grown, more fiercely burned
The smouldering flame, and ofttimes spurned
All semblance of control, and hurled
Me captive through a blinded world,
By passion madly driven. Yet came
Repentance oft, to nobler aim
That led. 'Twas in this milder mood
There came to tame my nature rude,
One, who as from another sphere,
Seemed but a stranger lingering here,
By Heaven commissioned me to bless
With brief but untold happiness."

### XXX.

" A revelation to my soul,
The influence of her soft control
Came like divinest airs, that blow
From Indian isles. I loved, and oh!
To love! 'tis Heaven! What soul can tell,
That never knew its blissful spell,
The transport that within our souls,
A burning tide of passion rolls:—
We, foster children of the sun,
Who live ten thousand lives in one!"

### XXXI.

Quick to his feet the soldier sprang,
And with each move impatient, rang

His arms, as with impetuous stride
He paced the rugged ingleside.
At length, as from some foe released,
By slow degrees his labor ceased;
And panting still, as he had done
Some deed of battle scarcely won
By potent force, he slow returned
To where the camp fire brightly burned,
And thus his waiting friend addressed,
Almost as he some fault confessed:
" E'en now, when burns the fire of youth
More tamely, chilled by years, in truth,
Through every nerve and vein, as then,
I feel its old time force again."

## XXXII.

He paused, then said with voice constrained,
As if the mere recital pained
His heart: "She my deep love returned;
But, for no cause apparent, spurned
My suit her father. Ne'er I knew
The reason; nor would humbly sue
For her, whom Nature made my own;
Who lived for me, and me alone.
We met in secret, and were wed:
Soon known the truth became. He said
No word, but in his look appeared
An evil spirit that I feared,—

Not for myself:—his tide of wrath
Might spend its force, ere from my path
By breadth of hair I turned aside;
But yet I trembled for my bride;
And strove his purpose to unfold,
With every art my mind controlled."

### XXXIII.

" At length one morn, with purpose fell,
Me he commissioned to compel
Submission from a lawless band
Of robbers, wandering through the land.
I sought their haunts with twenty men.
Through every mountain pass and glen
We rode, yet found no lingering trace
Of their abode.  At easy pace
Returning, careless of the way,
From ambush where they hidden lay,
Poured forth the foe a murderous fire.
My men, thrown in confusion dire
Scarce rallied, but in coward flight
Sought their escape.  In woeful plight,
One follower with myself remained,
Resolved to fight or die; but deigned
No further battle then to show,
Still hidden from our eyes, the foe.
Then turned we to our fallen friends,
To know if care might make amends

In those that wounded were to stay
Departing life. Save one all lay
In death's embrace. He strove to speak,
And though through loss of blood so weak
That scarce I heard, ere he expired
I learned that he for gold was hired
To be my murderer: the pretence
This journey was, to lead me hence
From home. Repentant now had he
Revealed the deadly plot to me."

### XXXIV.

" I heard with horror: yet belief
Came hardly. Seemed it dear relief
To see once more my loved one's face,
And there forget all deadly trace
Of crime; but, ere had sped the day,
New horror came, to chase away
The last. On that same battle ground,
Her sire, my foe, was murdered found;
Though by what coward hand he fell
Was mystery deep that none could tell."

### XXXV.

"At length, as whispered tales arose,
(We two were known as bitterest foes.)
Me for her mark suspicion made;
On every side my steps waylaid

With rumors, and dark hints, that hung
Like venomed poison from each tongue;
Till maddened by the false awards,
That pierced my soul like very swords,
I fled as from a living death,
Each moment that with fiery breath
My life assailed.  On soil of France
I landed first.  The broad expanse
Of waters, like a barrier rose,
Betwixt myself and hated foes.
Scarce safe from fear, with rapid flight
Came news that like a ray of light
My soul illumed.  The robber hoard
Subdued at last by victor's sword;
Their chief, now under just arrest,
Himself the murderer had confessed.
A base born hound, who for his wealth
Waylaid his steps, and struck by stealth,
All unawares, the fatal blow
That laid his haughty spirit low.
Yet following hard the short relief,
Came deep and agonizing grief;
For she,—my wife,—was dead, and died,
The self same day that o'er the tide,
Was wafted news of my release
From dread suspicion.  To increase
My woe, if ought could added be,
The child that had been born to me

With her was dead.   O lonely world!
As if from some high station hurled
Down, down, till far from haunts of men
By unseen forces driven ; and then
Of human sympathy bereft,
In utter desolation left,
My soul no comfort knew." Like bard,
Whose melancholy tones retard,
Then die away, he ceased.   St. John,
Himself moved deeply, mused upon
His words, while swift suspicion came,
That scarcely yet his mind could frame
In due proportion.   Every word,
Now with abated breath he heard.


### XXXVI.

" Came to me then, like knell that tolls
The requiem for departing souls,
Her loving words, that urged me hence
With tender plea in my defence.
" ' O love ; than life itself more dear ;
    Whose life mine own would purchase now ;
Yet must thou stay no longer here,
    To seal, with love, the lover's vow.
Thou know'st,—'tis for the pledge I bear,
That I thy peril may not share ;
But thou to distant land may'st speed
While unavenged the murderer's deed,

Till time shall prove thine innocence,
Mine own ;—O stay not!—speed from hence!
You white winged coursers, where they fly
On bounding keel, 'twixt earth and sky,
Shall bear thee swiftly on the way:
O haste! or else thy life must pay
The forfeit dread.   Fly! fly!—for me
Fear not: to know that thou art free
Shall be my solace; till that time,
When in some other, happier clime
We meet, and in that blissful day,
Shall love a thousand fold repay.'"

### XXXVII.

" O could the tongues of angels plead
For man, in time of direst need,
Then had I never left my own,
To wander through the world alone.
Then had I braved suspicion's power,
And stood acquitted, in the hour
That gave to crime its just award,
And on the murderer vengeance poured.
Then love had triumphed over hate,
And happiness inviolate
Had been :—but came such thought too late.
Remorse and bitter anguish came :
Then waked with tenfold power the flame
Of passion, blazing to the sky.
Almost the Heavens I could defy,

And sought to wreak on all mankind
The fierce revenge that filled my mind."

### XXXVIII.

" In war's rude toil relief I sought,
And like avenging fury fought;
For lived my wrongs in every foe
And recompense in every blow.
But rest came never; peace was fled,
And, save revenge, all else seemed dead.
At length in desperate fight were slain
My comrades all, and prisoner ta'en
Myself. In dungeon deep confined,
My spirit broken, not resigned,
Became a prisoner to despair.
Seven weary years I languished there:
The conqueror's death then made me free.
Released from bonds and tyranny,
Ere long I sought my native shore,
And reached my boyhood's home once more,
To find my rightful place had won
Another; image of the son
By wayward passions led astray,
Who fled to foreign lands away;
In many a battle fought and bled,
And was reported long since dead."

### XXXIX.

" And how,—speak truly—art thou named?"
St. John, with breathless voice exclaimed.

"I many names have borne: men call
Me rightly Henry Percival."
"And wherefore Lee?" "'Tis rightly mine,
Though not in strict ancestral line.
My mother bore it ere she wed;
From ancient sires inherited."


### XL.

" Then art thou truly that lost son,
Whose place, unknowingly, I won.
O hadst thou read the secret right,
When thou as stranger came that night:
How doth thy noble sire for thee
Still bear as tender memory
As when the fatal news first came,
That perished was his race and name—
Yet Heaven for all this grief doth send,
In Constance most divine amend,"—
"Oft and again her gentle face
Hath haunted me, with its fair grace.
And comes another, too, with eyes
Like hers; that once, 'neath southern skies
I wooed and won;—and loved;—but lost
Ere twice the sun his circle crossed.
Yet, for the love her memory bears,
And the regret, with love that shares
My heart, this gentle maiden fair,
Hath found her own sweet welcome there."

# CONSTANCE. 127

## XLI.

"I had a daughter once. Her name
Was Constance too; and she the same
In years as this fair maid had grown.
But her young life was early flown;
And in her mother's grave she slept,
Where both, with bitterest tears were wept."—
"Not so! In vain such tears were shed;
Hast thou no daughter 'mong the dead!
In Constance lives thine own, true heir;
Whose mother, dying, bade them bear
And place within thy father's care;
With charge that he the child should rear,
Till thou to claim her should'st appear."

## XLII.

"Oft have I heard the story told;
How, for accursed lust of gold,
Before thy sire his right could claim
In her, who only bears thy name,
The fatal news had crossed the sea,
That falsely told her death to thee:
And thou, ere could the truth be known
Beyond his knowledge long had flown,
Whom all these years he mourned." "Not dead,—
And Constance lives? O when had sped
My life in that dull prison, came,—
And then 'twas all I had,—her name;

And with the lesson that it bore
Brought back my faith, so long before
That left me : 'twas an angel's hand
That gave me life and bade me stand."

### XLIII.

" But while we linger here, away
By ruthless hands she's borne :—the day
Doth break anon ; why longer wait ?
On ! on !—thou still don't hesitate ?
But thou has never known the love
A father bears :" "Hold ! hold ! I'll prove
More than thou know'st : but prudence stil
Doth counsel some delay ; or ill
Ourselves, and those on whom depend
Success, prepared to meet the end.
Delay one hour ; and, as we may
Some rest obtain ; that with the day
Our plans matured, may full success
Ere long our every effort bless."

# CANTO V.

—o—

## THE CHASE.

### I.

The world sleeps on. Are hushed in brief repose
  Her children; who, oblivious of the day,
Alike forget their pleasures or their woes
  'Neath night's mysterious influence: but away
  With silent tread she steals; as dimly gray
The dawn appears; and roused to life once more,
The busy toil goes on, as aye before.

### II.

Scarce was the opening morn disclosed,
Through leafy branches that opposed
His path, ere from uneasy bed
St. John and Percival had sped,
And as on winged chargers flew;
But whither, e'en themselves scarce knew;
Save that with ardor unsubdued
They labored now to clear the wood.

At length, a welcome opening gained,
Their eyes with eager glance were strained
O'er the wide vale that tribute paid
To York's broad stream.   From distant glade
A solitary horseman came,
And towards them rode.   His arms the same,
And dress, as those they wore : his steed
High mettled, as he curbed his speed,
Chafed with impatience.   As he neared
Insignia of his rank appeared :
A herald's blazoned arms, that shone
His richly broidered vest upon.

### III.

Still nearer, halting, he addressed
St. John, who stood before the rest:
" Right noble greeting, brave St. John,
I bear to thee from Washington ;
Who bids thee, with convenient speed,
To hasten southward ; where 'tis need
That all his forces now combine,
Ere with the foe, in battle line
Is issue joined.   Two days I've sought,
And chance hath now our meeting brought.
Mine errand's told: I'll on."   " Yet stay :
Know that we seek, since yesterday,
A lawless chief, Glenwood by name,
Who late, with evil purpose, came

Where dwelt an aged man in peace,
With his fair child, for their release
Demanding one who there, he said,
Offender 'gainst their laws was fled;
But failing, made themselves his prize,
And now, we know not whither, flies.
Know'st thou of him?"

### IV.

    " Nought do I know
Of such :—yet, but few hours ago,
At little distance passed me by
A troop of horse, that seemed to fly,
As bent on some aggressive deed
That urged them on with utmost speed:
And now,—methinks,—and yet my sight
Might be deceived,—a palfrey white
Midmost I saw, a maid that bore,"—
"Then on! our quarry's still before,—
Yet, for thy words somewhat have cheered
Our hearts, much evil that have feared,
Kind thanks good herald,—on brave men!
Speed swiftly on! I breathe again."

### V.

Like cloud that flies before the gale,
Swept the bold horsemen o'er the vale,
And watched their rapid course the while
The herald, with contemptuous smile,

That grimly o'er his features played :
Then turned, reentering the glade ;
Doffed his accoutrements with care,
And stood once more the scout, Le Claire.
Then riding back, where Glenwood stood,
Just in the edges of the wood,
Said, pointing to the flying troops,
" See, to his prey the eagle swoops.
Now have we here a gallant chase,
Where the pursuer wins the race."


                        VI.


When the first beam of light that glowed
In eastern sky the morning showed,
Glenwood, with all his numerous train
Had left his hiding place, to gain
By path where he alone could lead,
The open country : for till freed
From the close wood where, hid secure,
Unnumbered foes might lie, unsure
Was every step; and sought he now,
With many a deeply muttered vow,
(Repentant of his hasty course
In taking from their home by force
His prisoners,) with the least delay
To rid him of their further stay :
For, till safe refuge was obtained
For them, he was perforce restrained

From challenge with the mortal foe,
So near that passed few hours ago.

## VII.

When gained the edges of the wood,
Well knowing he was still pursued,
He halted 'neath its thickest shade,
While issueing from a neighboring glade,
The scout rode forth the foe to meet,
As friendly messenger, to greet
With tidings from their distant chief;
That won, as we have seen, belief.

## VIII.

Beholding now from his retreat,
Where o'er the plain their coursers fleet
Far to the dim horizon bore,
Like ships that sought some friendly shore,
He onward with his forces sped
Where his pursuers swiftly led;
And all that morn their path he knew
By clouds of dust on high that blew.
But long ere night approached 'twas lost,
And when York's river they had crossed
No further clue the pathway showed,
Where with untiring speed they rode.

## IX.

Unhindered had their journey been
Throughout the day ; but now, within

The narrowing circle, where, 'twas plain
To thoughtful minds, that not in vain
The struggle* soon must culminate
In some fierce crisis, ere too late,
Was Glenwood minded to retrace
His steps; again his prisoners place
In their own halls, returning free
To aid the glorious victory,
That now, with sanguine hope imbued,
Not distant far his spirit viewed.
But confident, e'en over bold,
And well believing York could hold
Her own against invading force,
Resolved with still unchanging course
To hasten on, with brief delay
For rest. With dangers now the way
Was thick beset: on York were bent
All eyes, and centred there intent,
All interest through the land. The foe,
Assembled now to overthrow,
('Twas fondly hoped,) the kingly power,
Were closing round : if lost one hour
His forward move was checked ; retreat
Was vain, and nought but dire defeat
Remained : but with undaunted will,
His brave allies determined still

*The royal forces were encamped in and about Yorktown, while
the French and American troops were closing around them, in preparation for a prolonged siege.

To join, his further march he stayed
Until with swift approach the shade
Of night had come : then on once more
They moved, but slower than before.
Each soldier rode with sabre bare :
Each step was made with guarded care ;
And far the hours of night were sped,
And high the moon hung overhead,
Ere they had reached, where spread below
In even order, row on row,
Stood the white tents where slept the foe.
Still further back the city lay,
And gleamed the waters of the bay
Beyond ; where ships at anchor rode,
And dimly in the moonlight showed.


X.


With eager eye he scanned the ground
For safe approach, where circled round
With armies, lay the citadel
He fain would reach. 'Twas guarded well ;
But on the north, where York's broad tide
A shallow, marshy creek supplied,
He knew a pathway could be found,
That near the leagured city wound ;
And but that path in safety gained,
Might speedy entrance be obtained.

### XI.

At length resolve was ta'en.   His steed
He turned, and took himself the lead,
Descending to the river's bank ;
Then formed his troops in closer rank,
Gave short command, and onward sped,
With rapid pace, but noiseless tread.

### XII.

Night shone resplendent o'er the camp.
No more was heard the warder's tramp ;
Who lost in reverie mused of home,
And happier days that yet might come,
When war's rude weapons laid aside
Might gentler peace once more abide.

### XIII.

The river scarce one murmur gave,
Save when at times some larger wave,
With plash and ripple overflowed
Their pathway, as they onward rode.
The giant ships, whose mighty spars,
Like veterans of an hundred wars,
Loomed tall and ghostly, gave no sign
Of life : along the low, dark line
That marked the city, pacing slow,
The sentry watched for coming foe ;
Then halted, as his ear had caught
Some distant sound with danger fraught :

And listening, as the sound drew near,
Rang out his challenge, loud and clear,
" Who comes?" " Friends : 'neath the flag we ride
Of England;" Glenwood quick replied ;
And swept with all his followers past,
The wished for goal attained at last.

### XIV.

Each watchful sentry roused anew,
From lip to lip the challenge flew ;
But soon the welcome truth was said,
And save once more his measured tread,
No sound disturbed the silent night,
Till life returned with morning's light.

### XV.

Yet had his vision been more keen,
Could he, not distant far, have seen
Two horsemen, who their steeds had reined
And for few moments' space remained :
Then turned, and by a pathway steep
Toiled upwards, where with giant sweep
The bluffs arose commanding well
Far distant view.  Here they might tell
Each tent, e'en most remote, whose fold
Gleamed in the moonlight ; or where rolled
The river, mark each rippling wave,
And hear the lightest sound it gave.

## XVI.

A hasty camp had here been made,
And round about, within the shade,
(For still the mild September left
Some trees of covering unbereft,)
The soldiers slept, save one, who stood
As guardian o'er the solitude.
When reached the spot the riders two
To him their bridles lightly threw,
And sought their own repose, while spoke
St. John, who first the silence broke;
"Now have we tracked him to his den,
And when the morning breaks again,
Yon army roused in their defence,
We'll from his clutches bear them hence:
Then, till the night doth wear away,
To briefest rest,—if rest we may."

## · XVII.

Still following, as they thought, the foe,
We left them but few hours ago;
And still no further clue they found,
But by true soldiers' duty bound,
Their posts in battle sought to gain,
And hoped some knowledge to obtain;
St. John well knowing he could move
A thousand ready hearts, to prove
In such a cause their loyal love.

### XVIII.

By different paths, as chance ordained,
At midnight they the spot had gained
Where, shortly after, Glenwood viewed
The silent camp: but restless mood,
Ere his approach had further led
Their steps, and as with noiseless tread
He wended toward the river's shore,
And neared the city, swiftly bore
St. John and Percival behind;
Who, still to watchful zeal inclined,
Rode on, yet scarce with what intent
Themselves could tell. Their glances bent
Upon the river's gleaming tide,
First saw their shadowy figures glide
Along the shore: the sentry's cry
Had heard, and knew the voice that made reply;
Then backward turned, with hope elate,
The first gray beams of morn to wait.

### XIX.

As night's dark curtains slow withdrawn
Revealed the light, new hope to dawn
Began in either soldier's breast,
Who, roused from broken sleep, oppressed
By fitful dreams, glad welcome gave
To morn. O'er York's far-reaching wave
The mists, now tinged with roseate hue,

Slow parting, let the sunlight through;
Then rolled away like clouds of smoke,
As with increasing splendor broke
The glory of his rising beam,
And danced upon the glittering stream,
And tipped the hills with fire, and played
O'er trembling leaf, and hidden glade,
Till with electric life was filled
All nature, that with rapture thrilled
Beneath the magic touch of day,
And with one voice attuned her matin lay.

## XX.

Now, through the smoky wreaths upreared,
Tall masts and slanting spars appeared;
Then, as the clouds still lower fell,
Dark hulls loomed through the misty swell,
And active forms were seen to lend
United force, aloft to send
The sails, their dripping folds to dry
Beneath the clear October sky.

## XXI.

A flash! the nearest vessel speaks,
And floats from six and twenty peaks
The flag imperial of France,
Whose colors in the sunlight glance.
And hark! from Gloucester's distant shore,
With fierce reply, the lion's roar

Is heard, and waves in heavy fold
The royal standard, rich with gold,
Of England. With responsive shout
York rings her fiery challenge out,
And, answering to her brave ally,
Like emblem from her walls doth fly.
And back, where with converging sweep
Their sleepless watch two armies keep,
Rings out a welcome to the morn,
And flag of France again is borne
On high ; and near, fraternal waves
That flag, upborne o'er patriot graves,
A nation's name that gave the land,
Whose sons in Freedom's right here stand. *

### XXII.

St. John and Percival, from brow
Of distant mount beholding now,
Fired at the scene, with martial zeal,
At sight of war that soldiers feel ;
And, ere they hastened from the spot,
For one brief moment's space forgot
Their errand, and with loyal pride,
In shout that echoed far and wide,

---

*On the 28th of September, 1771, the combined armies of French
and Americans marched from Williamsburg and encamped about
Yorktown. By the 1st of October the line of besiegers formed a
semicircle, each end resting on the river, and the city was com-
pletely invested by land; while Count De Grasse, with the main fleet
remained in Lynn Haven Bay to keep off assistance by sea.

The soldiers led, who, at the cry,
Waved swords and plumed helms on high;
Then setting spurs they galloped on,
And ere another hour had gone
Had neared the camp, when sudden rose,
Like triumph hymn o'er conquered foes,
A slow, majestic strain, that clear
And musical came floating near
From rustic church, whose taper spire
Cast o'er the battle ground its shade;
Where simple priest and village choir
Their morning orisons now paid.

### XXIII.

As with instinctive awe they heard
The solemn hymn, whose every word
Full chorus wafted through the air,
They halted: 'twas the battle prayer.

### BATTLE PRAYER.

### 1.

God of Gods: to thee we pray:
Hear us on the battle day.
By thine arm the right maintain;
By thy power the foe restrain;
By thy gracious wisdom, deign
Us to guide,
Whate'er betide:
God of battles, hear.

## 2.

Lord of lords: to thee we cry;
Save us when the battle's nigh.
  By thy deep compassion aid
  Homes bereft and faith betrayed;
  Feeble age and helpless maid;
Over all
Let mercy fall:
    Lord of battles, save.

## 3.

Light of lights: to thee we sue;
Lead our hosts the battle through.
  By thy grace sustain and cheer;
  By thy presence banish fear;
  And in darkest hour be near,
Still to shine
With flame divine;
    Light of battles, lead.

### XXIV.

Died on the air the stately hymn;
But many a soldier's eye grew dim
With deep emotions, that diffused
In channels long till then unused.
Came from the door the thronging crowd,
And passed them by, nor spoke aloud,
But gazed, and turned to gaze again

With wonder, at the warlike men,
Who as their leader's voice was heard,
Roused them once more and onward spurred;
Soon reached the outposts, passed them through,
And 'twixt the allied armies drew
Their bridles   Cheer on cheer was sent
On high, and with loud echoes rent
The heavens, as passed that gallant band,
For every soldier in the land
Knew brave St. John, and his bold corps
Of troopers; welcoming the more,
For unexpectedly he came,
To lend the lustre of his name
And well earned valour, now to win
The battle that must soon begin.

### XXV.

Who, but with throbbing heart can feel,
And quickening pulse, the outpoured zeal,
That with spontaneous impulse springs
From thousand tongues to life, and brings
To one, who for the hour controls,
The tribute of a thousand souls.

### XXVI.

St. John, whose inmost soul was stirred,
Their echoing plaudits as he heard,
Doffed helm and plume, while rose the cry
Still louder, as he passed them by.

But, for their weighty errand now
No further hindrance might allow,
Both onward rode, till they had gained
The highest ground; their chargers reined,
And, leaping from the saddle stood
Where Washington his troops reviewed,
And, with his generals standing by,
The coming battle planned. His eye
Had marked St. John ere he drew near,
And had he heard the soldiers' cheer,
Nor wondered, for the soldier brave
Himself high commendation gave,
And gladly now, ere they assailed
The leagured foe, his coming hailed,
Whose prowess well their arms might aid.
Yet of his mind was naught betrayed,
By look or speech, till at his side
St. John had checked his rapid ride,
And with brief courtesy expressed,
Thus made, for both, his earnest quest:

### XXVII.

"O sire, ere doth the battle speed,
For brief delay and milder deed
We sue. Within yon city's walls,
Forth from their own ancestral halls,
By most oppressive force betrayed,
An aged man and gentle maid

Are held.  War 'tis unmeet to wage
'Gainst woman, or 'gainst feeble age;
And, for themselves the sight unmeet
Of battle.  Do we then entreat
That from our foemen thou demand
Their restoration to our hand.
As sons for a loved sire we sue ;
As father for a daughter true ;
And—more—" the soldier ceased: so high
His proud heart swelled: suffused his eye ;
And duller mind than his who heard
The truth had guessed, though unaverred.

### XXVIII.

Made he most noble answer then :
"Would that we waged not war 'gainst men ;
But woman hath a claim indeed
Most sacred.  Thou thyself shalt speed
With flag of truce, and in my name
To their commander urge thy claim ;
But haste ;—our work must be begun,
Ere high hath risen this morning's sun."*

*This incident is taken from an actual historical fact, thus re-
lated by Irving in his Life of Washington.  " Gov. Nelson, of Virginia, had an old uncle in Yorktown, who had taken no part in the
Revolution, and had no personal enmity to apprehend from the
English.  He had two sons in Washington's army, who were in
great alarm for his safety.  At their urgent request Washington sent
in a flag desiring that their father might be permitted to leave the
place.  Lord Cornwallis had not the inhumanity to refuse so just a
request."

### XXIX.

Within the city's walls, meantime,
Had briefly rung the matin chime;
And, called by roll of warlike drum,
Each soldier to his post had come;
While busy preparation rife,
Gave token of the coming strife.

### XXX.

At distance from the martial scene
Of half the town, that lay between,
Were lodged the prisoners, nor debarred
Their freedom; for each watchful guard,
On distant post his round pursued,
Or in the outer trenches stood.

### XXXI.

O'ercome with weariness now slept
Her grandsire.  Constance vigil kept:
Though wearied too, oft sought her eye
Through casement wide the glowing sky,
That told of night's departed reign,
And joyous day returned again.
Her ear had caught the distant drum,
And now discerned the mingled hum
Of step, and voice, and armor's clang,
And all the varied sounds that rang
Now near at hand, then more remote,
But ever with portentous note.

## XXXII.

Well suited to her pensive mood
Was the unwonted solitude ;
And well her fancy loved to stray,
 And picture, still the same,
That well remembered, happy day,
 When first her lover came.
Anon was wafted through the air,
'Mid warlike sounds a stranger there,
From neighboring turret's window high
A song, that came as from the sky.
Some prisoner, ta'en by war's mischance,
While gazing o'er the broad expanse,
Where from his prison stretched the bay,
Thus sang, to while the time away.

## SONG.

### 1.

For thee, my love, for thee I live;
And but thy smile its brightness give,
Though other light refuse to shine,
None other needs my soul than thine.

### 2.

Yet fairest maid, to thee unknown,
Lives in my heart that love alone :
And lips that fain the truth would tell
From thee must guard their secret well.

### 3.

But hope, e'en from a prison springs,
To soar aloft on happy wings;
And come that day or soon or late,
Unwearied still, my love can wait.

### XXXIII.

O hope! divinest messenger,
Speed on, speed on to comfort her;
So fair, so patient, who in chains
Of love and duty bound remains.
Ah! could she know that while she thought,
As if the very wish had brought
Her love, he to her rescue flew,
And nearer now each moment drew.

### XXXIV.

Scarce conscious, while she sadly mused,
Of a strange silence, that unused
Had hushed each sound, and now o'er all
The city hung like funeral pall,
Through the deep reverie of her soul,
At length with subtle power it stole,
And roused her, with a sudden fear,
As of mysterious danger near.
Assured that still her grandsire slept,
Up the broad stair she lightly stepped,
And reached the open roof, whence wide
The view was spread on every side.

## XXXV.

Far in the front the bulwarks rose
In varied lines, that kept the foes
At bay; beyond, the level field,
Where, curved in semblance of a shield,
In double lines the hostile force
Stood to their arms.  With rapid course,
Two horsemen now between them rode
With flag of truce, whose whiteness showed
But dimly, till they neared the wall,
And, halting, gave the bugle call
For parley.  Quick the answer came;
" Who hither comes, and in what name ?"
" In name of Washington we stand,
And by his warrant now demand
Two prisoners, who, unjustly ta'en
By lawless force, ye here restrain."
" By right of war we prisoners hold :
Hath thy commander been too bold
In making such demand."  "No claim
Have laws of war on those we name.
An aged man, whose silver hair
Marks him unfitted arms to bear ;
A gentle maid :—'gainst such as these
Comes England's army o'er the seas?"
" In cause of right," Cornwallis spoke,
" And honor, England never broke
Her faith.  The prisoners two are free,

And with safe conduct, now to thee
Shall be restored. My greeting bear,
Glenwood, to them, and here with care
Conduct them." With a brief salute,
Glenwood obeyed. His lips were mute:
But vainly might the pen essay
His heart's deep tumult to portray;
Where disappointment, rage, and hate,
In quick succession alternate.

### XXXVI.

Constance, the parley brief had viewed,
But could not hear, from where she stood,
The words that passed: and now, as near
Drew Glenwood, whom that night of fear
Had taught to shun, as dreaded foe,
She turned, and bent her steps below.
But when, with deference well feigned,
He his commission had explained,
And forth, with courteous conduct led,
Instant was all resentment fled;
And hope and joy beat high once more,
As swiftly towards the gate they bore.

### XXXVII.

And paint, if Nature's hand impart
Such skill, how each impatient heart
Of those who wait now thrilled with fear,
And hope, and love, whose wild career

Strange tumult made; and how the past
Was all forgotten when they met at last.

### XXXVIII.

Brief word was spoken then, while made
Full swift return the cavalcade;
And in a rustic cottage found,
(On outskirts of the battle ground,)
Safe refuge for the helpless pair,
Who found a kindly welcome there.

### XXXIX.

Scarce was the place of safety won
Ere sound of battle had begun;
And poured the leaguered city forth
In flame, like meteors of the north,
Red shot and shell, that fell like rain
O'er the besiegers; but in vain
Sought to provoke the like reply:—
    Nor gun nor cannon woke:
Nor sound was heard of cheer or cry;
    Nor answering volley spoke.
Each soldier at his post remained
    As if the fight was done;
Nor while the fiery tempest rained
    Was hostile act begun;
Save where in trench, with pick and spade,
Redoubled effort now was made,

As labored with unflagging zeal
The men, whose sinews turned to steel,
When from the city's walls before
Rang out the dread artillery's roar.

### XL.

With the first note of war, St. John
And Percival had hastened on ;
But halted midway to the field,
As higher ground a troop revealed
Of horsemen, o'er the plain that rode
With furious charge. An instant showed
That Glenwood led : an instant more,
As on with whirlwind speed they bore,
That vantage ground they sought to gain
Themselves to intercept. 'Twas vain :
For o'er the field, with thunderous roar,
  St. John's brave troopers spurred.
Like tempest on some rock-bound shore
  The rattling hoofs were heard.

### XLI.

With cheer, above the storm that rang,
To meet their foes the warriors sprang;
And met them in the midst, like shock
Of thunderbolt on rending rock.
Then 'gan fierce fight, and midst the fray
Hung even balance for the day.

Well matched in numbers and in skill;
Each fought as with demoniac will;
And blow of steel, and sabre's clang
Above the rattling thunders rang.

### XLII.

As from the cottage viewed the fight
Its inmates, trembling with affright,
In fiery combat closely pressed
Two soldiers, singled from the rest,
And with each blow still closer drew,
Till face and feature they could view.
Glenwood with furious passion fought;
Who from the first his rival sought,
Nor in the general strife had deigned
To mingle.  Percival maintained
His part with courage born of strife:
Nor battled for his single life;
But for the love, so late that came,
Of that fair girl who bore his name.

### XLIII.

Not long the contest was maintained
Ere Glenwood had the mastery gained;
But Percival, though wounded, still
Fought with unconquerable will.
St. John had hastened from the fight
To aid his comrade, when, with might

Concentred in decisive blow,
Glenwood unhorsed and hurled his foe
Stunned to the ground.  Scarce was the deed
Accomplished, ere with lightning speed
Sprang forth the sire, and seized the brand
Still held in his relaxing hand,
And full at Glenwood aimed such blow
As might have laid a giant low.
He tottered, from the saddle fell,
And the loud cannon pealed his knell;
And on the instant cried St. John,
" Now hast thou well avenged thy SON !"

### XLIV.

Then hastening back to make complete
The victory, in dire defeat
The foe was driven; and o'er the plain
The city's refuge sought to gain.
As stoops the eagle from his nest
High on some rugged mountain's crest,
And darts with fury on his prey,
Thus rose St. John's brave men that day,
And o'er the field of battle flew,
A living avalanche, that grew
In force and fury as they came.
And swept like fierce devouring flame
Their pathway.  With their foemen's dead
The bloody field was overspread,

And scarcely one remained to tell
Of those who in the conflict fell.


## XLV.

Meantime within the cot was laid
The wounded soldier, and essayed
Each healing art; but naught could stay
The life that slowly ebbed away;
And scarce the truth was fully learned,
Ere with quick step St. John returned,
Whom Percival addressed; " Good friend,
Scarce had we thought that this should end
Our quest, but 'twas not ours to say."
He paused, then said, " When yesterday
My life's past history thou woulds't know,
Part was forgotten, in the glow
Of sudden joy that came, like taste
Of waters in the desert waste;
But now with briefest word 'tis told:
In battle 'gainst invader bold,
It recks not when, nor where, two men
As comrades, though unknown till then,
Fought side by side.   One slight and fair,
A stripling, all unused to wear
The soldier's garb; his comrade, dark
Almost as Ethiop, bore the mark
Of hardy toil, and service done
'Neath many a storm and burning sun."

### XLVI.

" Like fierce, avenging fiend he fought,
And every post of danger sought;
And oft was singled by the foe,
As mark for skilful archer's bow;
Till pointed at his heart there came
One shaft with surer, deadlier aim,
That winged its way like flash of light,
When his companion marked its flight,
And interposed his ready shield;
But by the act almost was sealed
His death, for from the shield it flew
And pierced his helmet through and through.
He fell and from the field was borne,
But since that day the scar hath worn.
Thou know'st the man? Aye, THOU art he,
Nor canst deny." All wonderingly
His comrade's speech St. John had heard,
And now perforce its truth averred;

### XLVII.

" Not unremembered is the deed,
For now at times my sense doth heed
The wound, not soon that healed." " That scar,
That then thy lineaments did mar,
Now scarcely seen, at single glance
I knew, that night when seeming chance
As stranger to my father's door
Did lead me. Had I hoped before

My rightful place again to find,
And leaving all the past behind,
To live the years that still remained
In peace.   But otherwise ordained
A higher power.   Deep gratitude
Had long my inmost soul imbued,
For him who had my life preserved,
When that fell shaft, aside that swerved,
Made him its mark.   Unknown his name :
But when at length I homeward came,
And 'neath my father's roof him found,
My soul by every tie was bound
Of grateful love.   Thou art, in truth,
The image of my early youth,
And, startled by the likeness bold,
Scarce my disturbance was controlled :
But when I knew, resolve was ta'en,
That I unknown should still remain ;
And following to the battle field,
My life for thine might still be shield,
Till peace returned we two might come
As brothers to our common home."


### XLVIII.

Briefly he paused : but answer, none
St. John could make.   Himself had done
In that fierce battle, years before,
Heroic deed 'mid battle's roar,

An unknown comrade's life to save :
But he for him his birthright gave.
So nobly done, so simply told,
Scarce could the soldier tears withhold.


XLIX.

Again his comrade spoke : " The rest
Thou know'st: but little hadst thou guessed
My further secret. I was sent
On weighty mission, with intent
A lawless chieftain to subdue :—
Thyself the circumstance well knew.
Oft I before, with minstrel tongue,
The glorious deeds of war had sung ;
And once I sought in minstrel guise
His camp, and there, with strange surprise
Beheld—it were no shame to tell—
My brother in that chieftain. Well
He loved me in the past ; but long
'Twas changed ; for he of all my wrong
Is author. Both had loved the same
Fair girl, and mine was favored claim.
He knew not me, for my disguise
Had hid the truth e'en from thine eyes ;
And when his vengeful plan I knew,
Some rival chieftain to pursue
E'en to my father's halls, I fled,
And fearing for his safety, led

My forces thither: now, O friend,
All thou dost know, nor at the end
Think that *my* life was all in vain."
He paused, but instant spoke again,
" This morn I saw an eagle fly
Far up into the eastern sky,
To meet the sun.   His steadfast gaze,
Undaunted by the dazzling rays,
Pierced where mine own in blindness fell.
That eagle thou: with my farewell
Still onward, upward thou shalt speed,
Each day achieving nobler deed."

### L.

He took the hand that Constance laid
On his, and silent gesture made
St. John, who gave his own, and both
Were held in clasp that sealed their troth.

### LI.

Then, like soft ripple of the sea,
When some light wind breathes silently,
And o'er the glassy water flies,
The while the mimic wavelet dies,
Came one brief sigh, and all was o'er:
The soldier slept to wake no more.

### LII.

Now high his requiem be sung !
Yet how essay with feeble tongue

Such task.  His memory ever lives
Within their hearts, whose tribute gives
More fitting shrine than ever fame
Could lend to more illustrious name.
Then silently, with reverent tread,
Leave we the mourners with the dead.

With fleeting wing time onward sped.
When spring returned again were wed
St. John and Constance.  War had ta'en
Long flight, and Peace with gentle reign
O'er all the land held sway.  Once more
Their ancient homestead, as of yore
Free hospitality, to great
And small, despensed with former state.
And Percival, whose silver hair
More silver grown by weight of care,
Though still the same, his pleasure found
In ministry to those around
Whom, like himself, the war had left
Of one they most had loved bereft.
And as the years passed swiftly by,
With that fond love that could not die,
Would Constance oft the tale declare
To noble sons, and daughters fair,
Of how their grandsire fought and bled ;
Then showering on each sunny head
Full many a kiss and fond caress,
Would bid their tongues his memory bless.

## CONCLUSION.

### 1.

The minstrel ceased: but echo of her song
  O'er hill and valley seemed to linger still :
And in review, a swiftly moving throng,
    Created by the magic of her will,
    Passed on, as if her bidding to fulfill ;
Then vanished as beneath a broken spell,
As from her hand the silent harp strings fell.

### 2.

And was her art not all in vain essayed.
    Full many an hour had charmed her happier
      strain :
And for the sadder plaint sometimes it made,
    Yet nobler pleasure mingled with the pain,
    And tempered with a more heroic vein
What else had lived but for a summer's day,
And with the bare recital passed away.

**THE END.**